ktzttcsjhq iocagmlxug v'nxftjozw .

THE YOUNG
DETECTIVE

Stephan Pendley

A Love Letter to Myself

Prologue

There was something I wanted to do before this, but I'm afraid I'll never get around to it. I honestly don't know how to do this. I've never written one of these before, obviously. I assume most people keep them short and simple. Unfortunately, I have a lot to say. I just want to start by saying I'm sorry. I'm sorry to everyone I've hurt. Everyone that still cries tears to this day, like I cry every night.

When I was younger, I'd find myself laying around thinking to myself. I'd wonder of all the different possibilities my life would end up, places I'd go, people I'd meet, the one I'd fall in love with. I wish I had those days back. I find myself wishing a second lasted two so I could spend longer enthralled in those moments. Entranced in the better days for just a handful longer. Maybe I'd rethink it all. Maybe I wouldn't be such a villain. Maybe I'd actually have a life after this note is written.

I've caused so much pain. To everyone. I'm a rat, a burden, a liar, and a stain on humanity. But most of all, I'm a coward. I can't openly face the things I have done. I feel sorry for everyone around me. They look at me, see me, but they don't see ME. They don't see the anger, the hatred, the pain I've caused in the shadows. I am the phantom they don't know they hate. The villain they don't know they fear. I cry every day. For the last seven months I've done nothing but mope and cry. I can't go on. This weight, I will never push off my shoulders. My unforgivable sin. My guilt outweighs my will to live.

It should've been me. I should've burned that day. Burned then, and then burned an eternity more in hell where my black heart would rot forever more in the ninth circle. I wish I could take it all back.

I guess this is goodbye.

1

The Rain that Floods Norman

If there was such a thing as Hell on Earth, this was it for Jesse Rhodes: Norman, Oklahoma. Like the Indians of old, the wind danced across the plains; cold and bitter like the streets below. The gray clouds that overwhelmed the afternoon sky only served to make the city more...glum. *"God shines his brightness upon the good man,"* they used to say. There must not be a good man left in Norman, if that's the case.

The young detective, Jesse Rhodes, always found himself atop the roof of the NPD building. As if to find silence in the noise he couldn't escape. His head never stopped working. Like a ticking clock, his brain went on and on...and on and on and on. A blessing and a curse—best way to put it. Always thinking of how it was *all* supposed to play out. As if his life was some big storybook being written, and the conclusion was just one day away; all the pain he suffered was all leading up to one final moment.

Wind pushed and pulled his brown, straight hair across his face. His overcoat flowed in the breeze like a rolling black wool wave. From the roof, he could see all of Norman across the horizon. A shell of what it once was; like the rest of the damn country. What was once a lively, youthful town full of splendor, prosperity, and life had been gutted by the recession; nothing left but poverty, ghettos, and slums. Beautifully crafted houses were now drug dens, and office buildings were no more than places the homeless could cuddle up come the cold months. No amount of money could save this city's soul. It'd been ripped out and sold for a month's rent.

Deep in his thoughts, Rhodes looked over the city with the same dead eyes he'd had for nine years. He'd only been back home for seven months. It tormented him, greatly. Being back there in *that* city. It was like waltzing into the ninth circle with the devil himself. Day-to-day was torture for the young detective. But he had a job to do. He had a purpose there—a debt to pay. Right the wrongs of a day long passed and too soon forgotten. He owed them that at least.

In the whistle of the wind, it spoke to Rhodes like a wisp. Whispering secrets only time would reveal. Like warning. Jesse heard, but his deaf ears weren't ready to listen. He could sense it through the cascades of the breeze. *'Change'* he sensed. Something...something was about to change.

"The rest of us decided it was time to put your desk up here along with ya, son!" a voice spoke behind the young detective. Rhodes didn't bother to turn around. He recognized the distinct, hardy, deep voice tied together with a deep Oklahoman accent. "Clouds look awfully bad. How 'bout it? Tornado in December, ya think?"

Spurgeon Jordan. Everyone called him "Buck". Most people that knew him didn't even know his real name was "Spurgeon" the nickname was so prominent. Jesse didn't even know it was a nickname until he happened to notice the name written on his lunch bag his wife packed. He towered over most men, in height and in weight. The man never skipped a meal, or extra meals. Those suspenders that held up his black pants weren't paid enough for the work they put in. Jesse almost felt bad Buck had to walk up all those steps. Yet, he didn't know why he'd come up there with him.

Buck yanked the thick oval-shaped glasses off his pepper-bearded face and rubbed the fog off the lens with the flap of his coat. "Maybe if ya' wouldn't turn your phone off I can just call ya next time instead of havin' to walk up these damn steps." Buck said with a huff and a drip of sweat.

Jesse stood idle. As if Buck hadn't even come to interrupt his train of thought. Buck placed the glasses back over his withered, old eyes. Buck was a jolly, old man. The years had brought him nothing but happiness despite the line of work he'd gotten in. His knack was he could break a smile out of anybody. But not Jesse. He had yet to crack him. Like trying to make a cat bark, or a fish breathe air. He didn't know what to make of him.

"Have you ever seen a tornado, Jesse?" Buck came and stood beside him gawking at the sere sky.

Jesse gave a sideways glance to Buck. He wasn't sure if the part-time detective, part-time pastor was making small talk or if the question led to an omen. "No," Rhodes said. "I usually sleep through them, anyway."

"Yeah, well," Buck pursed his lips and clapped his hands together, "the idea—comin' through and ripping your whole life apart—just unsettles me. I don't sleep well during a storm."

"I haven't slept well since I came back," Rhodes crossed his arms together, still contemplating the clouds, the wind and the rain.

The wind spoke between them, and the rain echoed around them, but they didn't speak of it, again.

"Wolfe wants ya in his office—didn't tell me what for." Buck flung back open the door and proceeded down the steps with displeasure. "Damn steps. I'll be damned if I come up here to get him again. Make O'Massey do it!" he grunted to himself as he clung to the railing.

Before he acted, a few drips of rain trinkled down upon Jesse's face. Before the rain picked up, he proceeded inside. Not too long after Buck left. Within seconds he passed Buck going down the stairwell. He proceeded three flights and then entered the homicide unit of the station. The crowd wasn't flooded, most everyone was already off at home for the day. All that was left was Buck, Jesse and Sergeant Harrison Wolfe: Head Detective. The man was thirty years on the job; worked with the same three detectives on his staff for most of that time. Until seven months ago when Rhodes came in.

Jesse walked into the office. He eyed out the room as he walked in. Frames upon frames littered the walls; fishing photos, publicity shoots, awards, etcetera. On his ginormous wooden desk lay even more pictures. Not even one picture of family. Behind him were newspaper cutouts of famous cases dating back to early in his career. All the ones he'd solved. But Jesse was very adamant on one he *didn't* solve.

With his head buried in a newspaper cigar smoke rose over the pages. Jesse stood in the middle of the room. "You needed something?" he said in a still, calm voice.

"Sit down." Wolfe didn't lower his newspaper.

Jesse proceeded to take one of the two seats at the front of Wolfe's desk. Wolfe took his time before he lowered his newspaper, cigar in mouth, and revealed his wrinkly face. His eyes drooped even lower than his skin. The job aged him poorly. Like a wine that somehow molded in the cellar.

Both their dead eyes met each other from over the desk. As if to read one another, neither could guess the others next move; like playing chess blindfolded. The stare down was brief, but it was enough for both individuals to realize that the only course of action was to shoot straight with one another's words.

"The answer's no, Kid." Wolfe blew smoke from his mouth.

Fuck you. It's been nine years," Jesse retorted. "Don't you think some people deserve clarity in times like these?"

"Bringing this shit back up in the media is just going to spark hope—false hope at that. And if you don't deliver on some leads, which you won't; and make an arrest, which you won't, then you're just going to make everyone feel more hopeless. I'm doing you a favor, Kid." Wolfe laid his cigar in the ashtray and leaned back in his chair.

Kid. Jesse hated being called that. How demeaning, as if to spit directly in his face at the end of every sentence. It took every fiber of restraint not to lash out at the hearing of it.

"Leave it out of the press." Jesse said. "I'll speak to the families of the victims I know personally; I'll work on this alone. You won't have to worry about me."

"How long until people start talking that some detective is snooping around the Church Fire case? It'll be in the press within the week, and it'll be my ass and yours. We don't act until new evidence comes to us."

"There will be no new evidence! You fucks missed something all those years ago and ya let it run cold. Let me have this, Wolfe!" Jesse shot from his chair. The rage finding his eyes like an arrow to a bullseye. Wolfe stayed planted, snug in his seat.

"When you applied for this job, I read your file. Your name was oddly familiar to me, so I dug. It didn't take me long to figure out everything I needed to know—why you wanted *this* job, specifically." Wolfe leaned forward and stood up, meeting Jesse's gaze once again. "You only want this job to go poking your nose at *that*. No care for current events—what your job is—you just wanted to have a crack at it yourself. Nine years. You left this city, got an education in this field, just for this one moment. You've been here seven months; I see how you work a case. You don't give a shit about what you're doing. You're sloppy, arrogant, inattentive. And it's all because...you never wanted this job. You just thought it was the only way to get a look at that old case. For what? Closure? You're not the only one who didn't get closure, Kid. But at least you got something—something thirty children, police and EMT's didn't get—you got life. If you really want to do right by those people, good, start doing right by this department. Start worrying about the cases I assign you to."

The young detective let the words fall on deaf ears. He stood there, eyeing the man who'd just denied him his life's ambition. The one thing that woke him up in the morning; the one thing he laid awake at night obsessed over.

"Ya know what," Wolfe waved his hand, "I've been honest with you up to this point, here's a little more honesty: I never wanted you here. At all. When *Goodman* went missing a year back, I was more than happy continuing with just Buck and Shane. But they forced my hand. You weren't even my first pick. I knew this was going to be a problem from the start—all of *this* was going to be about *that*. You need to let it go, Kid. Get over it!"

"Thirty years. You've spent thirty years collecting dead bodies. It's easy to just let it go after you're done collecting evidence, aye, Wolfe? Just throw them in body bags and round up some druggie with a Glock .19? Well, Wolfe, those kids, those bodies you put in black sacks and kids you rushed to the hospital all burned to fuckin' hell..." Jesse walked up and leaned over the desk meeting Wolfe at the ear, "...those were my fucking friends. Not just some bodies. I'm never going to stop trying. For them."

"For your glory or for theirs?"

"You don't care, anyway."

Wolfe met Rhodes to look him in the eye again. "Don't think for a second I didn't give two shits about what happened that night. I would've given my life to put the ones responsible behind bars." Wolfe's face was stone, his eyes flooded with anger. He'd had enough of the Kid's mouth.

"But you didn't, did ya?" Jesse gave no sympathy to the man behind the desk. The man who'd Jesse felt, along with the rest of the detectives, let someone get away with burning thirty-one kids alive and severely burning twenty-seven more. That's why he showed no compassion for them. That's why he loathed being in their presents. Day-in and day-out he soaked deeper into his hatred for them.

Jesse didn't say another word. He let himself out of Wolfe's office. Midway through the doorframe, Rhodes paused. Eerily, he turned his head downward looking back at Wolfe with his peripherals.

"Next time hell comes through Norman, you'll be the one that gets burned," said Rhodes with grit in his voice.

"I'm already burned...more than you, I'd say."

Rhodes let himself chuckle. The young detective slammed the door behind him, rattling the pictures on the wall.

2
A Cup of Tea

The rain poured as thunder clapped across the murky sky. Soaked, Jesse persisted the mile or more walk to his apartment on the southside of town. Stormy weather did not bother him; his mind was on his next move. One way or another, he was going to reopen that case. If it meant breaking the law, Jesse was prepared.

Though the conversation was brief and frustrating to him, Jesse still heeded Wolfe's words. *Sloppy, inattentive, unmotivated.* In the seven months he'd been a detective, he'd worked three murder cases. The first one, rather an open and shut case; a dealer hacked a "client" of his over a debt owed. Witnesses didn't rat him out, but the guy just so happened to leave more than a dozen fingerprints, the murder weapon, and his shoe at the crime scene. And a mile down the road during his getaway, his wallet fell out of his pocket—dealer seemed like he used his own product.

The second one, some decayed body found in one of the plethora of abandoned buildings across the city. There wasn't much to go off. Some DNA under the fingernails is what ended up identifying a killer.

And the third one was just some weird sex thing that went horribly wrong, for the woman, at least. Whatever keeps these druggies occupied since there's very little work to go around. Why not go out on top? Well, she was on bottom, but that isn't the point.

During those three investigations, Jesse was attentive. He paid attention—left no stone unturned. Took notes, made sure every microscopic cell of evidence was collected. He also noticed that his fellow detectives... well, they did fuck all. Stood around the crime scene, all of them, just eyeing the body as if it were a spectacle—something to gawk at, not to investigate. Buck would make some half-witty comment about the body, O'Massey would chuckle, and then they'd bicker over which bar they would go to later in the night. How could Jesse be so "sloppy" if he was the only one putting in effort?

"Bastard." Jesse mumbled under his breath. Not as if there was anyone around to hear it if he were to scream it to the heavens. He spoke under his breath the most—his true voice, he'd say. If life was a game of chess, words were the pawns, and those pawns needed not be frugally spent on insults—no matter how good it would feel to say.

Wheater it was next week, or fifteen years down the line, Jesse was re-opening that case, somehow. It was his life's devotion. Nothing else mattered. Not some random murder case; that wasn't to be his life's work.

That case. He swore to avenge his friends. Or die trying—whatever it took.

By the time Jesse made it to his apartment door, he was soaked from brim-to-heel in the unforgiving Oklahoma rain. As brutal and chaotic as the weather was in the plains, it didn't compare to the storm that bellowed inside the young detective.

The door to apartment #336 groaned as he threw it open. There wasn't much inside but the essentials. A couch, a TV, a refrigerator, washer, dryer; no personal knickknacks or hobbies lying around, merely the things that were needed.

The beige walls were cracking and molding. The insides crawled with bugs. But, given the circumstances, it was labeled as one of the "nicer" additions in town. With the state of everything, that isn't really saying much.

There wasn't much for Jesse left to do but plop down on his rugged couch and contemplate, think...dwell. Not with any alcohol to ease the pain of it (he refused to drink anymore) just sitting alone with himself and that dreaded mind.

Flashes of blue followed by shrieking rumbles lit up the room through the blinds. All the city and the metro was getting rattled by the storm. Tornado season was a few months away, but tornados come and go as they please, and leave very little left behind. One could spring out of the sky at any moment and devastate any area it so well felt like. Ripping through houses and plowing through fields—killing thousands. A tornado and *the* fire were the same to Jesse in that regard: it took so much, and left so, so little.

Maybe a tornado would rip through tonight, he thought. Suck him up and rip him to shreds along with the apartment. *What good am I dead?* He asked himself. *Then my life will have been in vain...just like theirs were.*

There was little in the cabinets to eat. The shops—the few that were still left—had very little to store. If it wasn't bread or milk, they most likely ran out of it years ago. All that was readily available was what was grown locally. They only way to make any sort of living was through the neighborhood markets—trading and selling goods. But, for Jesse, it was a can of beans for dinner.

His mother dabbled in making homemade beans, usually cooked with bits of pork, almost every night for dinner. Just one more reason to hardly visit. They were repulsive to him; the look, the smell, the taste. It reminded him of when they were growing up and all they had was beans while the rest of his friends were at home dining on chicken fried steaks and fried bread. But now, everyone was dining on beans, so Jesse was more used to the feeling of poverty than they were.

With a knife, Jesse punctured a hole and ran it across the brim. He folded the piece of tin back and turned the can upside-down letting the slop ooze its way into the bowl below. With disgust and disdain, the young detective ate up.

Standing at the kitchen island he sloshed the beans across his tongue while his mind ran and ran and ran, and then ran some more. All the different steps he could take just to bring justice to a person he did not know. A phantom which had alluded him for seven years. An enemy without a face. But Jesse didn't need to know his face to ruthlessly hate him with every cell inside him.

After finishing the beans, and washing the bowl and spoon, Jesse started off to bed. Before he could even flick the lights off, he was interrupted.

Knock, knock, knock...

Jesse never had visitors. Not even his family down in Noble came to visit. Especially with the thunder and rain, no one should be seeing him. With hesitation, he unlocked the first bolt and then swung the chain off the notch. He recognized the person that very second. He wasn't expecting to see her; that night or ever again.

She'd gained a healthy bit of weight since they last met eyes. Her hair was back to its natural brown rather than the faded crimson dye. Her cheeks were rosy and plump rather than sunken in like a blanket draped over an open box. She was dressed head-to-toe in black—make-up and all. Without invitation, she walked right into the petite living room of apartment three-three-six.

"What are you doing?" Jesse scoffed as she walked past him.

Allaura Ellis turned to meet Jesse eye-to-eye. "You've been back seven months and didn't say anything?"

"What was there to say? I haven't seen you in five years. How'd you know?" Jesse stepped closer to her—a fire swelling up in his eyes.

"Your mom. I saw her the other day. You should really go see your parents more, dude. They miss you." Allaura looked up at him with a sense of gentleness in her gaze. Jesse tried not to look into her green, orbs. Still, after all this time, they had an effect on him. The hooks to his sutures.

"Been busy. Work is work. People don't just stop getting murdered on the weekends." Jesse sighed. "Do you want to have a seat?"

"No." Allaura said. She reached into her coat pockets and pulled out white tea bags. "I brought makings for tea; do you have a pot?"

Jesse pointed to the cabinet in the kitchen. "Sit down while I make you some," Allura said grabbing a pot.

"Allaura this is my apartment—"

"Sit down...while I make you...some tea," Allaura gritted, gesturing to the couch.

Jesse wiped the tiredness from his eyes. He sat down as the girl he once knew pranced around his kitchen. She filled the pot with water from the faucet, boiled the water, then hung the teabags over the brim. Scavenging through his cabinets, she found the last bit of sugar and mixed it in with the boiling syrup. All while he eyed her. He knew this wasn't just a cordial visit. She wasn't plotting to be reacquainted...she needed something. Allaura filled two cups, steam rising from the glasses, and brought them over to the living room. "I made sure to add as much sugar as possible. Just how you liked it: with a little extra diabetes."

He took a small sip, not breaking his gaze off her. Allaura had a light smile on her face, and seeing it rubbed Jesse the wrong way. He didn't remember what her smile looked like. "Tastes too sweet."

"First time I've heard you say that," Allaura said.

"What do you want, Allaura?" Jesse put the cup down on the table, leaning over the cup so the steam could rise to meet his senses.

"Why do you assume I want something?" Allaura fell back in her chair resting her head in her hand. The smug smile washed away by the crass questioning.

"I haven't seen you in five years. And now, on some random Tuesday, you show up and make me sweet tea?" Jesse took another sip.

"Thought you just said it's too sweet?" Allaura smirked.

"Never said it was a bad thing. Now, answer my question." Jesse demanded after a gulp.

"I haven't seen you in so long," Allaura rose in her chair. "I just felt...like maybe it was time to see you again—see how you were doing. You come back to Norman, you get the job as a detective, I wanted to catch up."

"So, my mom told you I was a detective." Jesse said.

"Yeah. Yeah, she did." Allaura cleared her throat. "I-I think that's great, Jesse. I know that's what you wanted to do."

"What've you been up to?" Jesse asked, a rather dull tone in his voice.

"I work at station four up in the city. I've been firefighting for nearly three years now. It makes me feel more *at one* with myself, ya know?" Allaura looked down at the floor.

"Better than what you were up to." Jesse sighed.

With a sigh, "It's been an uphill battle," Allaura replied.

Jesse rose from the couch, grabbing both cups. Allaura still had a gulp left in hers. The glass cups met the bottom of the kitchen sink, rattling as they hit. Allaura sunk farther into her seat as Jesse walked back into the living room towards her, his gaze dead-eyed and shallow.

"You're here for a reason," Jesse stood over her, "Tell me."

Allaura felt uneasy, but she knew him well enough he wouldn't dare harm her physically. She inhaled a deep breath. "Please sit, Jesse." He walked back to the couch and sat down.

"So..." it didn't take long for Allaura to fall teary-eyed, "about a year ago, a little less than that...we found Dad in his office. He was hung off the ceiling fan."

Brent Ellis. Jesse remembered him as one of the toughest men he knew. He towered over everyone. He started off as a cop in his early twenties, and by the time he retired, the man was chief of police. He was there the night the fire burned, pulling kids out like his life depended on it. Ran into that burning church without an oxygen mask or any sort of fire-resistant suit. Still wore the burns until the day he died.

"I can hardly believe it." Jesse couldn't wrap his head around it. "What made him give in?"

"I don't know." Allaura's eyes glazed over looking at her feet. "We were supposed to go visit family in Dallas three days later...but, yeah."

"Said this was a year ago?" said Jesse. "Why didn't I hear about it?"

"I don't know. The funeral was fucking expensive, though. We're still paying it off—we're barely getting by." Allaura started fumbling her hands.

"Is that what you need? Money?"

"No. I would never ask you for anything like that." Allaura got up and sat with Jesse on the couch. She scooted in close as she pulled something out of her coat pocket. "This picture is of Dad's office, before he died."

She passed the photo over. The young detective observed. Brent, in the picture, was smiling at the camera sitting down at his elongated oak desk. His hands were sitting on top of the desk, burn scars as visible as day. Behind him was a bookshelf with a safe under it next to white curtains to cover the windows—nothing out of the ordinary.

"So," Allaura's voice choked. She rose her shaky hands up to her face to wipe her eyes, "We'd just got back from the marketplace—I traded in my old bike for a half gallon of milk—he was alive and happy when we left. And then we get back twenty minutes later, and he's hung from the damn ceiling fan."

"You left, and when you got home, he was dead? Who all was in the house?" Jesse asked, still looking at the photo.

"We all left. My mom, my brothers and me. He was the only one left at the house. It just doesn't make any sense!" Allaura gasped as emotion overcame her. She took a moment to compose herself. Jesse sat there, not relaying any sort of comfort, waiting for her to regain herself.

"Why'd he do it?" Jesse asked. "You think maybe all the troubles over the last few years got to him? You think maybe a druggie daughter and a family to feed while the world's gone straight to hell finally got to the man?" Allaura's head shot up. Through the tears, a stare of piercing anger met Jesse's cold, dead eyes.

"Don't be an asshole." Allaura grabbed Jesse by the right forearm and rose it up as if she was showing him something. "We all grieved in our own way, Jesse. It was just as hard for me to watch you as it was for you to watch me destroy myself; day-by-day." She threw his arm into his lap. Jesse, still with a dead expression over his face, showed no reaction to her words.

"Get on with your story," Jesse suggested.

"When we found him," Allaura continued, "His safe was wide open—nothing in it. I reported it to the detectives but a few days later they ruled it a suicide. They never even investigated the empty safe."

"Maybe there was nothing to investigate." said Jesse.

"No! He was so uptight about that stupid safe. He wouldn't even let *me* or *mom* know the combination. It couldn't've just been empty all this time." Allaura exclaimed. "They missed something. Jesse, I don't think Dad killed himself. I think someone made it look that way."

"You think it was murder?" said Jesse. "And what exactly do you want me to do?"

"I don't know. I assume you have access to case files. I just want to see if you can look into it. Maybe, reopen my dad's case if need be—if you find something."

Jesse thought for a moment, cascading his eyes across the floor. Allaura tracked his eyes, a speck of hope filling her soul. The young detective stood up and made his way towards the door. He stung the door open and then looked back at Allaura as if to say, *"Get out"*. She winced in disbelief, but she wasn't going to pry him any further. But she couldn't help herself. "Jesse," her voice crumbled, *"please."*

She walked slowly towards the door, looking him in his soul through his black-hearted eyes. She didn't feel the warm loving embrace she used to feel when she looked into those green eyes. Her voice filled with anger as she walked through the threshold of apartment three-three-six. "Jesse! After all I've done for you, just this *one thing*. You owe me!"

"Owe you?" Jesse leaned against the door. "The last time I saw you, I drove you to the hospital with a needle in your arm. You were *this close* to dying if it wasn't for me. And then, after all that, I visited you in the hospital...I told you I loved you and you laughed at me. No. I owe you nothing."

Allaura opened her mouth as if to say one more thing, the words she didn't dare let slip out. Jesse slammed the door bashfully. His legs gave way, overcome with emotion, he fell against the door sinking to the floor. He looked up at the ceiling, he felt emotion try to overtake him. Within himself, even in the solitude of his own home, he wouldn't let himself express any sort of weakness. "So," his voice cracked, "that went well..."

3
Can't Let it Go

It was cold when she arrived, but it was colder when she left. Rhodes collected his thoughts, he threw his bowl and his cup in the sink and tried to sleep. But, as many nights before, his head was flooded—restless—with mystery.

Firstly, he couldn't believe Brent had been dead this whole time and no one bothered to mention it to him. Not even his mother. Though, his mother knew he wasn't on good terms with Allaura, so what good would it had done for her son? Secondly, Wolfe open-and-shut the case? This made no sense to him. As far as he knew, there was some repour between the police chief and the head detective of the Norman P.D. They were friends, Rhodes believed, so why wouldn't Wolfe have brought it up Rhodes always thought it was Brent who convinced Wolfe to bring him in to fill Goodman's spot.

It just doesn't make sense, Rhodes' mind kept wondering to itself. To the point where the prospect of sleep became a useless endeavor. Jesse found himself making coffee at two-thirty in the morning. He grabbed his laptop and started reading articles relating to Brent's suicide. He knew it was bound to have droves of attention.

The first article he read headlined: **Police Chief Found Dead in Norman Home!** Jesse read the full article in under a minute; no mention of the safe or really anything Allaura had mentioned. Just the cut'n'dry rundown of the family discovering him in his home office. Sad ordeal, really.

    Rhodes knew it couldn't've been easy for Allaura, especially. Not just because she'd lost her father, but with the overwhelmingness of it all, it could've sent her into a relapse, Jesse thought. From what Rhodes deduced, she looked healthy. None of those grizzly-looking track marks he'd see begin to pile up on her arms when they were teenagers. And when he'd question her, she'd lash out. Jesse's innocence got the best of him. But it all came to a head one night when he went to take her out of a club there in Norman and he found her overdosing on the floor.

    All those scantily-dressed people, just dancing over her pulsating body, foaming at the mouth, with a needle in her arm. The memory was imbedded in him forever. It was the second scariest moment of Rhodes' life.

    Rhodes got up the next day to the sound of his buzzing alarm. He'd fallen asleep with his laptop on his chest, tabs of articles still open on the desktop. Out of all the articles, he found nothing on the open safe. But what else he'd collected? Wolfe didn't even wait twenty-four hours before telling the press it was suicide.

Must've made quick work of it, he thought.

Rhodes decided to walk to work that day. The air was chill, and the fog hazed the road. He could see far enough in front of him to know where he was going, but that was it. The gray skies had decided to dance on the plains that day.

It was a slow day at the office, as expected. No murder meant dreaded paperwork. Rhodes couldn't stop thinking about the Ellis case.

Rhodes went down to Records and pulled the file. The receptionist working the desk, Rashanda, handed it over to Rhodes with a smile, "I remember hearing about that one. Crazy stuff."

"If only it was that easy to pull the Church Fire records," Rhodes said, bitterly.

Rashanda looked away from him, confused, then walked away from her desk. Rhodes went back upstairs and sat down at his desk. The first page in the file was the autopsy report. "Self-conflicted asphyxiation." The photographs weren't an easy sight for Jesse to look at. Brent's body was pale, his tongue slightly drooped from his ajar mouth. His neck bent sideways resting on the noose. The rope was knotted to the ceiling fan just above the desk.

Behind the desk, Rhodes could see it plain as day: the open safe. It was open well enough to see what lay inside it: nothing. Completely empty.

Odd, he thought. But he wasn't going to ask anyone about it. Who was there to trust? Buck? Buck would feel some sort of divine conviction and fess up to his God—meaning Wolfe. O'Massey? Rhodes couldn't decide which he hated more: his shit-eating grin or his pompous remarks.

Better to it keep to myself, he thought, observing the other two detectives across the room buried in paperwork.

Rhodes continued skimming the file. Still, nothing more to question besides the ajar safe. At the end of the day, Jesse took the file back down to Rashanda. "Best not tell Wolfe about this," Rhodes made clear.

"Hold on," Rashanda waved her hand as Rhodes was walking away.

"Yes?"

"That Church Fire case you mentioned," She began, this immediately caught Jesse's attention.

"What about it?"

"It got checked out over a year ago."

Rhodes neck jolted. His mind was sprinting, suddenly. "By who?"

Rashanda went to her monitor and typed in a combination of numbers. "...*Goodman.* Jeff Goodman."

The man Rhodes replaced. The one that just up and left and didn't tell anyone. Buck had told him all about Goodman.

What was relayed to him: Goodman went down south—some small town off the highway to Dallas, and he never came back. Didn't tell his wife or daughter anything. They never found his car, or any trace that he'd stopped in been there that day. Everyone assumed that, due to financial hardship, he just kept driving and made it down to Mexico.

"Shit," Rhodes said under his breath, "Thank you for that."

Rhodes drove back to his apartment, festering. He couldn't wrap his head around any of it. Of all people to have the entire case file! Jesse felt compelled to beat in his T.V.

Bowing his head and staring blankly at the floor, Rhodes let his head run; trying to make sense of it all. *Wolfe must've been too proud to tell me,* he brooded. "Incompetent fucks!" He shouted, alerting the neighbors.

But as his anger simmered, his thoughts begged the question: Wolfe, in their conversation said he didn't even want to hire Rhodes after Goodman "went missing". But Buck told Rhodes that Goodman "up'n'left". *Then which was it?*

The young detective shook his head, *perhaps I'm overthinking.*

Suddenly the prospect of solving the case felt hopeless. Everything he'd dedicated his life to had been an impossibility from the very beginning. His whole adult life had been for nothing.

Rhodes went to his bedside table and grabbed a photograph. He looked at it with so much heartbreak welling up inside. Most of the kids in the picture with him were long dead. And the ones that were alive were visibly scarred and disfigured. Maybe Rhodes would seek to join them, soon. There was nothing else he could do.

It was late into the A. M., and Detective Rhodes was still beside himself. Laying, curled up, on the floor, lights on and his eyes wide open. Only one word spun around in his head: *Hopeless.*

To break his concentration, the phone rang abruptly in the living room. Rhodes almost neglected to go answer it. But whatever mustard seed of will he had left compelled him to get up and answer it. He put the phone up to his ear and a familiar voice sounded on the other end.

"Hey, Kid," said Wolfe. "Head on over to Beaumont Street. We got a body."

4

Beaumont Street

Without any more insight, Wolfe disconnected the call. Jesse, rubbing his eyes, rolled off the couch and scrambled back on his tie, shoes, and peacoat. "Fuck," he muttered, sprinting out of the apartment, not remembering to lock the door behind him. The weather, after the rain, fell to thirty degrees. The chill hit his face and hands like a stinging shrill—he paced to his car. The roar of the engine could wake everyone in the complex as he turned the key.

Beaumont Street. It wasn't more than a hop, skip and a jump from Jesse's place. It was on Eastside where all the crazies lived. Eastside, even before the recession, has been riddled with Wack jobs, loonies, and people that were just down-right mentally ill. The Norman Asylum was located just up the road from the neighborhood street in question. For the longest time, an entire section of the institution was abandoned, but with everyone losing money, the facility shut all its doors for good. And where were all those poor mentally unfortunate people to go? Back onto the streets...just like Beaumont Street. Druggies, Crazies, and many, many more; that was Norman, now.

From the main road, Jesse could see the red and blue flashing lights blaring from the little side street. There wasn't a single car on the road passing by him, he noted. He didn't see anyone walking up the sidewalk. Jesse turned onto Beaumont to meet the battalion of police cars, firetrucks and ambulances already crowding the tiny, brown-brick cottage where he noticed Wolfe and Shane O'Massey starting to walk in.

Jesse didn't know the neighborhood at all, or who might've lived there. He had to park at the street sign. Neighbors and onlookers and news-reporters had already crowded the perimeter of yellow tape. Cops stood guard on the other side making sure no onlookers got *too* curious. Jesse proceeded to walk towards the scene. He stuck his nose down and his ears up listening to the scrambled murmurs.

"Goddamnit," exclaimed a woman.

"Who lives there?" asked a voice.

"I didn't hear anything," a man's voice said, "and I live right there too!"

Jesse moved through the crowd, pushing people out of his path. He made it to the yellow tape and flashed his badge to the cop guarding. The cop lifted the tape for him as he passed, all while giving him a look that Jesse read as: "It ain't a pretty sight in there."

"Jesse!" a woman's voice from the crowd exclaimed. Suddenly, Jesse felt a hand grip his left forearm; he batted the hand away quickly, his eyes bulging from his head. He turned around; he knew the woman. The last he'd seen her, she had a lot less wrinkles on her face. "Mrs. York," Jesse collected himself.

"Is that my baby in there?" Her eyes filled with worry as the streams flowed down her cheeks.

Jesse went to church with one of her daughters, a girl named Carrie York. They weren't that well acquainted with each other, but they ran in the same circles. "Ma'am, I don't know anything, I just got here."

Mrs. York covered her face and dropped to her knees. The stress had gotten to her. She fumbled over herself as the cops on guard duty instructed her to get back. Jesse proceeded up the steps, to the porch. He grabbed a pair of latex gloves; there was a box of them just outside the threshold, and then entered the house.

The reek hit Jesse with just a step in the doorway. O'Massey and Wolfe were standing in the living room conversing closely with one another. Jesse could read eyes like books. He caught a glimpse of Shane's brown gaze as curiosity struck him to who'd just walked in. Wolfe was explaining something; he peered back over his shoulder. Jesse could tell they were calculating something. As if the look he gave them spoke sentences, it said "We've got to play our cards right."

Jesse turned to one of the EMTs that was making her way out of one of the backrooms down the hallway. "Where's the body?" he asked as she passed by.

"Down the hall—backroom." she said in a hurry, rushing out the door.

Jesse didn't wait for anyone's go-ahead. He made his way down the hallway with cautious determination. He could see flashes from the backroom, where forensics were taking pictures of the scene. With every step, the stench got stronger. Before he even walked through the door, he could see what he was there for.

Two bodies. Both were already gray and brown with decay and decomposition. Their hairs were greased and frizzled as it drooped down, half-hiding the nooses around their necks. They were tied to the base of the ceiling fan. One chair lay tumbled over behind them representing their final action. The noose looked fresher than the bodies did. They were light brown as if they were switched out... or tied around their necks after they were dead.

In the room to the left side was a queen-sized bed with a wooden frame. Nightstand on both sides, the bed was neatly made. To the far-right, a tv and dresser was found undisturbed. Next to it, another door which led out to the side yard.

Walking towards the bed, Jesse noticed an envelope laying on the left nightstand. He looked down at it, observing the red lettering. Written in janky handwriting with bold letters, on the envelope itself it read: "**Acknowledge ME**". The inside of the envelope had no note. Just the two words.

Wolfe and O'Massey walked into the room. Jesse heard their heavy footsteps. He turned to them, pointing to the letter. "Y'all see this?"

"We've been here an hour longer than you. Of course, we've seen it." Shane replied.

Jesse placed the letter back down properly how he found it. He went back towards the bodies. From their decomposing faces, he couldn't tell if he'd known them. But with the encounter with Mrs. York outside, he knew as least one of them; and by that he could only guess the other.

"Mrs. York's girl?" Jesse exclaimed.

"The one your looking at. Elizabeth York. And the other one is her girlfriend—"

"Lola Everett. Yeah. I knew them." Jesse interrupted.

"Take away their gold stars?" Shane snickered.

Rhodes shot O'Massey a dirty glance. Shane chuckled to himself.

"Cut it out, will ya?" Wolfe interrupted.

Wolfe walked around the two bodies and met the young detective. Looking into his gaze as if to see how attached he was to the victims. But, he came to find, the young detective just had that consistent, emotionless expression.

It was true, Jesse knew them. They ran in the same circles growing up. They all knew *of* each other, and they were friendly, but they weren't close. He knew them from church and saw them around school. Growing up, the two girls were thicker than thieves—inseparable: even to their death. Both grew up in the foundation of Christ, which made it even more shocking news when they came out. It wasn't as big of a shock to the community or their church family—it's not like they hid it well. But, gladly, their families were supportive and didn't treat them as outcasts or monsters. "They were in the fire." Jesse blurted out.

"I thought I remembered their faces by their ID's." Wolfe glanced up at Ms. York. "So, you did know them?"

"Kinda, sort of." Jesse examined their necks. He noticed on Elizabeth the bruising around her neck wasn't consistent with the noose whatsoever. the bruising was above the noose entirely, the young detective noticed.

"How tight is this noose?" he asked.

"Tight enough to do the job," Wolfe replied, "clearly."

Jesse moved the rotting hair to the side and pointed at the bruising. Wolfe looked up at his gloved hand. O'Massey's eyes darted to Wolfe. "You're telling me at some point her neck shifted out of the noose?"

"I'm not telling you anything, Kid," Wolfe scoffed. "Good eye, though. You mind going back outside with the mother? Maybe we can figure out why they off'd themselves."

Jesse winced, "This is too sketch, Wolfe. You can't be convinced they did this shit to themselves."

"Couple of lesbians living in the heart of the Bible Belt? Nothing to eat in the fridge—probably barely affording this place. Come on, Jesse—open'n'shut." O'Massey beat in his point. "I mean, I'm sure even the homeless devil worshipers on southside got it better than this."

"This has nothing to do with that," Jesse walked and picked back up the note, "Acknowledge ME? Me? Why not 'Acknowledge US'?" Jesse walked back over to the bodies. "No... something's up here."

Hung by the neck... that sprung something up in Jesse's memory. Something he'd just heard about earlier that night. Something that he'd just been researching minutes before he'd gotten to the crime scene. "Brent Ellis died the exact same way."

Shane's eyes darted to Wolfe. His pale skin flushed red. Wolfe nodded at him as nonchalantly as possible. As if to say: "stay calm."

"'The fuck -you know about that, Kid?" Wolfe blurted out.

"I knew him better than to off himself. It doesn't make sense—"

"Kid, go home. You're imagining shit. Go give the mom your condolences and fuck off. I don't need your speculative bullshit on this case. It's a suicide." Wolfe's voice raised.

"What the fuck did you just say to me?" Jesse turned his whole body to Wolfe, stepping towards him.

Shane stepped toward both of them. He was a bit taller than He looked down at Jesse putting a fat-fingered hand in between the two. "Watch it." he said.

Wolfe didn't break eye contact. Neither did Rhodes. "There's something more going on here, Wolfe. And I think you know that."

"That little sweetheart of yours is in your head. We worked that case. Now, fuck off. Call Buck on your way out—"

"HOLY SHIT!" Shane fell back, as did Jesse and Wolfe.

The bodies had been there six days prior to their finding. The fan that was dangling around three-hundred pounds from it had finally given way. Violently, the fan ripped out of the ceiling and the two girls fell to the floor, their lifeless bodies flailing. Green and brown flehm oozed from one of the victim's mouths. The body that found itself on bottom made an eerie elongated gasping noise—all the built-up gas being released. It was as if she was calling out—screaming—one last time.

It was a sight that would stick which each man in the room. The ugliness of death. Everyone, in their heads, has an idea of how gruesome murder and death can be...but no one really know for sure until they've seen it for themselves.

The three detectives in a moment forgot about their grievances. They all backed away from each other, mostly to stand back from the bodies.

"Call Buck yourself," Jesse looked back at Wolfe.

Jesse walked out. The EMT's and forensics were filing in-and-out of the living room and porch. He ripped the gloves off and threw them on the carpet floor. They landed next to a piece of candy wrapper—the only remanence of clutter in the house.

Walking past the tape and back to his car, Jesse felt a hand grab him and swing him around. It was Mrs. York. "Was she—"

"I'm so sorry." Jesse put his hands on her sides. The woman couldn't contain herself. She collapsed on the Kid. Her yells of grief could be heard five streets away. The crowd that had gathered around the police tape had suddenly all turned to the whimpering woman. She'd pulled Jesse down to his knees as she curled up on him, beside herself.

It didn't faze him. Not a single bit. It was like his mind had come to take tragedy in as a normal happening—nothing to be emotional about, just what life itself had succumb to being: tragedy after tragedy. He stared blankly at the slab of sidewalk, letting the poor woman have her upheaval. EMT's rushed over and pulled the woman away and gave her the "shock" treatment. She fought them the tire away, pulling on Jesse's suit and peacoat. "I'm so sorry." Jesse grabbed her hand one last time, letting the paramedics whisk her away to the back of an ambulance.

Rhodes got in his car, roared the engine and sped away back down Beaumont Street. "FUCK!" Jesse punched the steering wheel with the base of his palm. There weren't any cars on the road that dead into the night; he sped past every red light. From the trip back to his apartment he saw one car speeding the opposite direction of him.

Nothing about any of it made any sense. The note, Brent, the girls. It's like they each correlated with each other yet correlating them made absolutely no sense. It rattled Jesse's brain. He knew, in his mind, it made sense, yet; it made no sense at all.

He stumbled back up the steps to his third-story apartment. He knew he was going to hear it at length when he went to work in the morning. He pulled his keys from his pocket and as he was just about to unlock the door, he stepped back. The knob was completely off the door and laying on the ground. He immediately grabbed his sidearm and yanked it from its holster. He pushed open the door with the fury only Rhodes could have, ready to shoot any and all burglars. His living room was completely trashed. The couch and chairs were flipped over, the TV was on the floor of the kitchen, the rug was ripped up, the food was ripped from the refrigerator; milk poured across the kitchen floor, and the door to his bedroom was ripped from its hinges.

Jesse cleared the house. Not an assailant in sight. Whoever it was, they were long gone. "Son of a fucking BITCH!" Jesse yelled, possibly waking a neighbor or several. Jesse's bedroom was the same. The mattress was thrown from the frame, and the stuffing and springs were ripped from the confines. He stormed back into the living room. Even though the apartment was completely trashed, he noticed nothing had been stolen, as if it was targeted. So, I couldn't have been some druggie looking for cash or valuables.

In the living room, atop the toppled couch, an envelope sat rather neatly. His heart sank. For a moment, he thought Allaura had come back while he was gone and went ballistic. But the second he noticed that envelope...he clinched his gun tighter. He grabbed a napkin from off the floor and picked up the envelope. It was empty of a letter, but on the closed side in bold, red letters was a single-worded message. And suddenly, it all made sense. Everything put together, in a moment, was correlated:

"Dig"

5

Pauls Valley

Dawn broke, gleaming into apartment three-three-six through the half-ripped blinds. Jesse didn't clean a single inch, neither did he call the police to report the break-in. He sat there, crept in the corner, and contemplated the message. *"Dig"*... the word taunted every cell in his brain. But, somehow, he knew what the word meant. As if an omnipotent presence was overseeing him. He knew what he had to do: get to the bottom of it. The suspicion he'd had, within himself, was proven right.

Darkness wouldn't let him sleep. When daybreak arrived, Jesse's mind lulled. He was always in the office by eight, but when he woke up it was half past eleven. He staggered through the mess. Groggy from his unpleasant sleep, he drove gingerly to work. His hair a mess, his tie loose, and his eyes weighted down by the bags underneath. He could hardly keep his head up. All his mind could think about was that car. The one he passed on his way back to his apartment. When his headlights showed on it as it sped passed him, for a moment he made out what color it was. It was a light beige, like an old seventy's grocery-getter. But beyond that, he didn't remember a single detail. He didn't have a clue what Allaura drove or if she even had a car. But, a part of him, was certain she wasn't the vandal that broke into his house. But he had to play it easy. His cards had to be dealt correctly to the final ace. The young detective was alone on an iceberg surrounded by a Wolfe and his hounds. His next moves had to go undetected. Like a phantom in the darkness.

    He stumbled into work like a man with a hangover. He rubbed his eyes as the lights from the office struck him. Outside was still gray, like it always was on the plains in the winter months, which made the lights even more intense. He staggered up to the third floor where his office was. In the main lobby, full of empty desks and sprung-about papers, the three lovely detectives which Jesse admired oh, so much were all lounging around conversing. Buck, deary-eyed as Jesse, was leaning back in a spinning chair. Buck was no small man. Jesse couldn't help but think about how that chair was performing an act of God to keep that man from falling over. With a hardy laugh over something Shane's smart-ass mouth said, the wheels on the bottom creeks as if to call out to whatever deity would hear their cries.

    As the door shut behind him, the three noticed Jesse enter. "See you finally decided to show up," O'Massey taunted.

"I didn't get much sleep," Jesse began, "Your wife needed me to fill her box last night. Thanks for giving me the night off, Wolfe."

"Ah, asshole, I ain't married!" Shane proclaimed.

"I guess that was your mom, then. Bet you want to lick my fingers, don't you?" Jesse replied.

Buck nearly fell back in his chair. His laughter could be heard from the basement level. Red-faced, he said, "That'll shut ya' up, wont it, Shane?"

"Yeah, well, at least I'm not late to work." Shane retorted.

"Man, I'm so damn tired I'd wished I'd just slept the mornin' in. Give ole Juanita some lovin' before I had to come and sit in his hell-heap for eight hours. Ain't much to do 'round here, anyways."

"What about the case that came in last night?" Jesse said. "We still have to work on that."

"Well," Wolfe interrupted, "You're not on that case, even if it were a case to begin with, Kid."

"You can't tell me there wasn't something off—"

"We found both girls' notes under the bed. They probably just forgot to put it in the envelope before they committed. Open-and-shut."

"Let me see the notes." Jesse demanded.

"Don't worry about it," Wolfe said with a smug look on his face. "I have something else for you today."

Wolfe waved the young detective into his office. Buck and O'Massey got disturbingly hush. Rhodes took note of that. He walked into Wolfe's office behind him, shutting the door.

"I hate to admit this, Kid," Wolfe began, standing behind his desk, "*You're right.*"

Rhodes raised an eyebrow. Wolfe gave him that same dead, unreadable look he'd had on his face for forty years. "Something's going on here," he continued, "I need your help."

Rhodes wasn't sure to mention his apartment being trashed, if that wasn't confirmation enough. He didn't even know how to bring up the note he'd found in the same ink and penmanship as the one found in the Beaumont house. What all this could mean.

"About time someone else caught on," Rhodes said, slyly.

Wolfe sunk into his swivel chair, palming his face, his eyes closed with an elongated sigh. "Kid, I've known for a while something wasn't right. The world forgot about our problems. We have as little resources as any department did a hundred years ago. Left to defend ourselves like dogs fending off dogs. Nothing about the world makes sense anymore."

"A part of me wishes I could disagree," Rhodes began to slouch, as if the weight of the world was falling on him during the conversation.

"What I've come to find is the only way to make it any better is to only worry about what's in your control. I'm no messiah, I'm not going to lift an entire country out of a depression. But...but I can look out for my own." Wolfe nodded, looking blankly at the desk.

"What do you need from me?" Rhodes felt a sense of poise.

"What'chu know about Pauls Valley?" Wolfe asked.

"Not much," He remembered the rumors about Goodman. Suddenly it was all linking together.

"It's one of the bigger rural areas in the South-central. It was lucky enough to be settled just off the highway heading down Dallas-way," Wolfe reached for a file in his desk drawer and presented it to Rhodes. "Go to this address. Don't tell anyone where you're going. You'll know what you find when you find it."

Rhodes took the file and opened it. On a sticky note over the police report was a handwritten address: *111312 North County Road 1100, Pauls Valley*. The young detective couldn't believe his eyes. He couldn't believe he was actually coming one step closer after being stagnant for so long. With a nod, Rhodes left the office and made his way through the hall.

"Hey, Jesse," Buck called in a bass voice only a preacher man could muster.

The young detective turned to him. "Buck?"

"Let God guide your steps today." said Buck with a pleasant smile. The kind of smile a proud grandfather would give.

Rhodes just nodded his head and went on. The drive down south was too long to worry about one of Buck's omens, anyway.

Sitting down in his car, just about the rev the engine, suddenly Jesse felt uneasy. His chest fell into his stomach, his palms sweaty. He felt a strong need to make sure he was prepared. Rhodes fumbled through his black peacoat and jacket and placed his hand on the handle of his pistol. He pulled it from its holster, took out the clip, and counted the rounds within. He counted eighteen shots. He reentered the clip and placed it back in his holster feeling a bit more at ease.

Backing out of the station, the tires squalled alerting of his departure. Somewhere inside the station, Wolfe was staring into the beyond with a look that could only be deciphered by the ones that truly knew him. From his car, Jesse could feel the eyes looming over him like an angel following overhead. But if anything, Wolfe was an angel of death, leading him to his untimely demise.

"Dig", the word bounced in his mind. The note was snug in his pocket. He could feel it shift and hear it crumble with every turn on the wheel. As if it were trying to whisper to him. Not letting the young detective feel void of its presence. The winds that brushed across the plains didn't speak as loud.

Jesse knew once he returned from this, his mind would be focused on nothing the two girls. They deserved better than what Norman had given them. Nothing could change what happened, but it was up to Jesse to make it right. It was the weight he carried on his shoulders. Every day, he took it upon himself to re-write every wrong done. No matter how improbable that was, he wouldn't stop until it was made right.

But, still, nothing to him made sense. It was all scattered puzzle pieces jumbled across the floor. Those girls had been there decaying, rotting, festering away for six days before they were discovered. Yet, the second their bodies are found, his apartment is trashed with the same note and handwriting.

As main road turned into backroads and the city was long at his back, that rattled his brain. Flatlands and cow fields surrounded his path. Deer and buffalo roamed the fields, gnawing at the lush grass under their hooves. Jesse wished life was that simple—just a deer in the fields. If only God had been that kind to his children.

"They were watching us," Jesse murmured to himself as he passed yet another cow field.

But he couldn't tell that to the others. They'd already shut the case. *Poor, Mrs. York,* Jesse thought, *She'll never know the truth. But why? Why would you murder these girls? Why would Wolfe cover it up? How is Brent tied to all this? How the hell am I tied to all this?*

None of the pieces connected in his brain. The puzzle was still scattered on the ground. To maybe connect some of the edges, he brought it all back to the Church Fire. The basepoint for where his life began, and others ended. Did they know something, Jesse begged the question, *did Brent know something too? And whatever it was, was it worth dying over?* That brought his mind's eye back to the safe Allaura had mentioned. It was emptied out.

Allaura, his thought process came to a halt. Still stuck on the girl he used to know. The second she entered his mind, she wouldn't let the thought of herself pass. She stuck there for miles more down the road leading into Purcell from Lexington. Over the bridge a hundred feet from the ground overlaying trees and fields with a stream running through it, he held onto that broken bond. He hated himself for it. He couldn't stand her yet all the while he couldn't stop thinking of her. A "mindfuck" as they call it. She was his kryptonite. But he'd never let her back in. Not after what happened.

After thinking a million-times over different scenarios that could've--in his mind should've--played out, he shook his mind's eye back to the case at hand. *The safe,* Jesse sighed, clutching the steering wheel as he came to a red light in the town of Purcell. There wasn't a car on the road but his. All the residents had boarded up their homes and hardly ventured out due to all the looting and pillaging going on. The schools had all shut down quickly into the recession. The only people Jesse saw lurking about looked whizzed out on some drug or crawling around helplessly for a crumb to eat. It was saddening what the world had come to. Only the lucky survived. And even luck was scarce.

Allaura did trash my place, young detective entertained the thought, s*he waited for me to leave, came back and wrecked my apartment... but I didn't leave for another five hours.* She couldn't have scoped out my place for that long. But that doesn't explain anything else. Not Wolfe, the safe, the matching letters, The Fire, the double murder, the cover-up.

"It's too messy," Jesse rubbed his brow coming up on the outskirts of Purcell. To his left was a tin-roofed building which was once a diner. The gravel parking lot had gone unkept along with the building. It was caving in on itself. To his right, nothing but trees, country and fields. Jesse sped down the winding backroads out in the middle of nothingness. Out there, man was truly free. Not in their cities or their suburban homes. Not in their bars or clubs; but out in the lands. Where nothing *was*, not even law. Just man, nature, and his nature, whether it be civil or beastly. He wished he could just escape out there. Ditch the badge, the car, the gun, and all of what he had and just escape into the open plains. But too much was at stake for him. Also, his mother would worry sick. He couldn't do that to her.

He sped down the winding roads at nearly ninety miles an hour. The only thing around to stop him was the roadkill that laid in the ditch every quarter mile. Deer, skunks, opossums, armadillos, and several raccoons all lining the pavement and the ditches. Vultures swarmed the skies above, descending upon their fill of rancid meat. Poaching animals seemed to have their bellies full more than people nowadays.

    In no time the young detective had sped into Wayne. Even before everything had gone to shit, not a soul could be seen in Wayne. When Jesse was young, they'd guess a number before entering the town. If they saw the number of people equivalent to the number they guessed, they won the game. Choosing one, two, or zero was always the safest bet. Jesse couldn't help himself. As he came upon the "Welcome to Wayne; Blink and You'll Miss It" sign, he picked a number in his head: *Three*—rather bold of him. Jesse flew through the town with a lead foot on the gas pedal. He saw not a single person; his guess was all too bold.

    Ten or so miles of country and train track separated Wayne from Paoli. Paoli was a mile in every direction. Nothing there but a park, a few houses, an abandoned school yard, and plenty of druggies to make the town worth a damn. The only thing you needed to know about Paoli: that's where the young detective Jesse Rhodes investigated the "weird sex thing" murder. Easy to say that venturing through the town once again left a sour taste in his mouth. It was like being over at his parent's house; he could name a million other places he'd rather be.

Jesse made sure the mile stretch it took to reach the end of town didn't take longer than necessary. After seven more miles of countryside and farm fields, he'd reach Pauls Valley, Oklahoma.

There wasn't much to say about the town. Just like any other small town, it had its old buildings and old shacks here and there. And between those shacks? Churches and cornfields and cows... The address Wolfe had given Rhodes was obviously a back road, most likely on the very outskirts of town. As far out in the middle of nowhere as any man could possibly get. Rhodes found it best to go into town first and find someone to give him directions.

The only gas station that was still up and running had a broken sign dangling from its post. The white paint had been chipping away for years, it seemed. Rust crawled up the side where a mural of a thunderbird faded away.

The young detective walked in, a bell sounding off as he opened the door.

A pepper-bearded man lounged behind the counter. The place reeked of dust and old sewage. The hot case on the front counter was turned on but not a single morsel was being heated on it. Guess just to keep the old man warm, Rhodes guessed.

"What's the price of gas this far south of the metro?" Rhodes asked.

"So damn much you'll wanna walk back home, jus' 'bout," he said. "Near seven dollars for jus' a damn quart!"

"In the city its eight-fifty for the gallon," Rhodes leaned over the counter with a grin.

"No damn sense, none of it—no damn sense!" the man rose his voice and flailed his arms.

"How much for law enforcement?" Rhodes flashed his badge.

"No different," said the man, "If a pig wants a discount, quit making the price of bacon so damn high. Shit, I pay so much 'n taxes I'm pretty much buyin' your gas already!"

"I can't argue with that," Rhodes could barely contain his laughter, "how long v'you lived around here?"

"Went to school here," said the man, "and you ain't gotta be no detective to know for me that was a long-ass time ago!"

"Then you're just the man I'd like to talk to," said Rhodes taking out the file and showing him the sticky note with the address written on it.

The man glanced up at him with a worry in his eye, "Whatch'u want all the way out 'there?" he questioned.

"Police business," Rhodes replied.

"Yea..." the clerk handed him back the note between his two fingers, "Pull out this lot, take a right, keep goin' down on that'a way, you'll make a left up at the ol' schoolhouse. If ya miss it ya got shit in your eyes."

Rhodes reached into his wallet and pulled out a bill and placed it on the counter. Not to purchase anything, just to say thanks. But the clerk behind the counter was still glaring at the young detective like he'd seen a ghost.

"You know what'cher getting into out there, now?"

"No. Not exactly." Rhodes headed for the door.

The directions were clear enough for Rhodes to follow. The drive down to the old schoolhouse was ten minutes through clusters of cattle and corn. The abandoned schoolyard was home to overgrown grass that climbed up weathered field posts. The white-brick schoolhouse had vines growing up the building almost to the flat roof.

Concrete turned into gravel at the turn onto North County Road 1100. The road started downhill through woodland. There didn't seem to be much out there.

Right before Rhodes came to the end of the stop sign, he found the address. It wasn't an old shack or an abandoned house. To Rhodes' dismay, of all things, it was an old church building.

The last time Rhodes stepped on holy ground, it was burned to a crisp, littered with dead friends. He never forgot the sight; burned in his memory, you could say. The building looked untouched for years. The roof was caving in on itself and the vines, like the schoolhouse, crawled up the outer walls like centipedes. The front door laid broken in the entranceway; the frame had been ripped off along with it.

Rhodes clutched his pistol. He didn't want to get surprised by any druggies lurking about the place. Upon stepping over the broken door, the smell hit him like a truck. A smell like rotten flesh and bludgeoned intestines. The aroma forced the young detective to gag, nearly losing his breakfast.

Inside the church, the burgundy carpet had nearly turned a blackish remanence. The cross that once hung on the back wall lay broken on the floor as the structure lost its integrity. The pews were still aligned facing the pulpit, dust and debris collected across them.

Flies attracted to a singular spot near the front of the church. Rhodes cautioned every step. He leaned his head to try and see over the pew as he got closer. Pointing his gun, he leapt around the pew.

"Poor thing," Rhodes said, slyly at the sight of the decaying dog.

Rhodes put his gun at his side with a sigh of relief, but also a sigh of aggravation. He still didn't know fully why he was down in the middle of cow country. He stumbled around the church, growing nose blind to the smell. He stood at the top of the pulpit, the light from the windows all piercing his eyes. It took him a moment to get used to the glare.

Then it struck him: a bullet.

As he peered out the window, his eyes caught on to three men with automatic rifles pointing them at the church. They moved in unison as they fired entire clips into the church.

    Rhodes fell to the ground elevated by the pulpit. The bullet pierced his right shoulder as the automatic rounds deafened him. He bear-crawled down the stairs feeling the skin and muscle rip even further. He found cover under the front row pew.

    The young detective's heart raced; blood left a trail on the floor as we made his way further down the line of pews. Gun in hand, he stopped crawling towards the midsection. The sound of empty clips was ringing in his ears. His breath was spiritic, the adrenaline pumped through him numbing the pain of the bullet. He was lucky to only be struck once.

    The quiet was too quiet. Rhodes peaked his eyes over the pew down the walkway. He couldn't hear their footsteps the ringing was so loud. But, to his advantage, he could see their shadows advancing on the entrance way.

    With his offhand, Rhodes pointed his gun. His eyes locked on the entrance. The first man stepped through the door, scanning the pulpit. He didn't even see the young detective peering his head out from under the pew. The mistake cost him—Rhodes shot the man through the head; brain matter painting the fallen door red.

Rhodes knew he had to move. He could hear the other four muttering, not expecting the deadly blow. As they cursed and screamed just beyond the door, Rhodes staggered to his feet and ran to the front row pew where the dog lay.

The two entered spraying the pews with bullets. Rhodes curled in a ball, but it wasn't enough to dodge another round from grazing his hip. The bullet took the wind out of him, he gasped in shock. The sound of shots ringing halted, and Jesse knew he had to act.

The men broke off and started clearing in between the pews. Rhodes rolled over facing the dog carcass. Footsteps crept closer to him. He heard them nearly over top of him. Rhodes shot up, knowing that this was not his day to die. One of the assailants was two rows away from him. Rhodes shot the man twice; once in the jaw, the second time in the neck.

Without a moment of reprieve, the last man lunged at Rhodes, bringing him to the ground. His pistol flew from his hand. The lead bullet still in his shoulder cut deeper with every movement. Before the young detective could cry for help, two hands grasped his neck with a murderous squeeze.

His face turned red, he grasped aimlessly for his gun, but it had fallen over the pew. Rhodes could feel his life draining, he was moments from passing out, his life leading up to nothing. In his head, he contemplated how much of a sick joke it all was: all his friends dying in a church, him dedicating his life to avenging them, just to meet the same fate years later. No, Rhodes wouldn't allow it.

With a last valiant effort, Rhodes grabbed the dog carcass and smashed it into the man's temple. With a wince and dry heave, it was enough to thwart the assailant off him. Rhodes gasped for a much-needed breath. The job wasn't done. He flung his body over the man who was reaching for his rifle and hit him over the head with the skull of the dog. The exposed teeth caught him in the brow drawing blood from the cut. After two more hits, the dog's body detached from the head, and Rhodes was beating the man with the skull as if it were a stone.

The man's arms flailed, trying to gain control over Rhodes, but with all the rage of fifty innocent lives behind him and one swift blow to the temple, the man lost consciousness.

With the high adrenaline and intensity of the situation, Rhodes didn't realize the man was out of it. He kept wailing and wailing, and screaming until the man's skull nearly caved in. Weeping, Rhodes fell over beside him realizing the fight was over.

Weeping turned into hyperventilating. Rhodes picked himself up still grasping onto the dog skull as if someone else was going to jump out of the shadows. Over the bodies, Jesse staggered out into the lot. He tripped over the steps causing more pain in his shoulder and hip.

His bloody hand fumbled for his keys while he staggered to his car. His head was fuzzy. He couldn't correlate his fingers with his brain. Grabbing and reaching acted more like picking and prying as he tried aimlessly to put the key in the keyhole. Rhodes leaned on his car door for stability, nearly falling on the gravel lot. Blood smeared the black paint of the door.

Just as Rhodes managed to get the door open, he heard the roar of a diesel engine. Rhodes fuzzily looked up and saw a truck coming down the gravel road right toward him. He knew he was done for. He had no fight in him, his eyes were going dark.

Rhodes leaned against the car sinking down onto the pavement, blood pooling his clothes. He tried to cry out for help, but with his body shot up and overwhelmed, he managed a gasp before finally passing out...

Informing the Family

Seven-seven eighty-three Fox Lane. Wolfe pulled up to the house made of red brick in a neighborhood on the outside of Noble, a town just south of Norman. Shane O'Massey scoffed at the sight of the house. It wasn't run down or beat up, unlike almost every house in Norman, it was who the house represented that the old brat didn't like.

"Fucking Noble," O'Massey hopped out the car as Wolfe veered to the curb, "explains a lot about that kid, eh?"

"Stay quiet, Shane," Wolfe walked around the car, "let me do the talking."

Dawn had barely broken over the horizon. As the morning sun glistened through the trees, and the hue of blue gray muddied the air, Detective Harrison Wolfe knocked three times on the burgundy door, "Police Department!"

A minute rolled around, stifling, and the clammer of feet shuffled towards the door. Slowly, to avoid the obnoxious creaking, a petite, frail-looking woman answered the door. "I have sleeping heads! Don't knock so loud," said the woman adjusting her glasses to get a good look at the two men of that wished to speak with her.

"Excuse us," Wolfe brought his fedora down from his head to the base of his chest, as if to appear as welcoming as possible, "we're here to speak with Margie Rhodes."

"That's me!" Ms. Rhodes exclaimed with a thick, Georgia-southern accent she'd inherited from her southern belle mother.

"May we come in?" Wolfe asked pointing his head down, "It's about your son, Jesse."

Ms. Rhodes swung the door open for them, her heart sinking into her stomach. "Follow me into the living room, y'all," she exclaimed.

She led the two detectives down the hallway, the walls covered with family photos, into the back of the house where the living and kitchen were. "I was just making coffee," she said going to the kitchen, grabbing three cups from the cabinet.

Wolfe and O'Massey stood in the center of the living room peering at Ms. Rhodes. Awkwardly, Shane fumbled his hands around, his face flushing pale. Wolfe stood with a blank expression—emotionless. As stern as a bear eyeing the river for salmon.

"I'm assuming you work closely with my boy," Ms. Rhodes poured the coffee and offered it to the men. The two detectives took the cups and sat down at the edge of the woman's couch.

"I was the head of his department," said Wolfe with a sip.

"He doesn't come around here often," she admitted, "I guess he's always busy cleaning up murders and what not."

"He does his job well," Wolfe replied, "When was the last time you saw him?"

"Well," she began, "about three months ago, I'd say. I had him help me arrange my furniture—he wasn't too thrilled, but I enjoyed seeing my baby."

"Ma'am, did you hear about what happened in Pauls Valley yesterday?" Wolfe leaned forward, close enough to touch her leg.

"Oh, good Lord, yes! How awful! All those poor men and their families." Ms. Rhodes let two-and-two click together in her head, her eyes finding the ground in discomfort, "He wasn't down there, was he?"

"Ms. Rhodes," Wolfe began, "we just got word your son was found dead this morning."

"Oh, my word..." Ms. Rhodes nearly dropped her cup, "You're telling me *he* was down there?" Tears already began to fall before Wolfe could even continue. Her hands started to shake as she pulled them to her face.

"Yes, he was." Wolfe continued, "I urged him not to go, but...."

Ms. Rhodes dropped her cup on the brown carpet. The coffee splashed and a bit got on Wolfe and O'Massey's shoes and pant legs. O'Massey held back rageful curses, not as if his clothes were clean. Wolfe stayed in the same manner as the Kid Detective's mother broke down on her living room couch.

"*My boy*," she whimpered, "my baby boy!"

Wolfe reached into his coat pocket and pulled out a card, "If you need anything from us, please feel free to reach out," he placed the card on the arm rest, "The Police Department are holding a memorial service for him this upcoming Tuesday. I take it you'll be there?"

Ms. Rhodes kept to herself. She heard the words he was saying, but her grief was overwhelming. She'd loved that boy, through it *all*. She'd loved him from the moment he was born. Praying for his protection and his redemption every night. And at that moment, she did not know if he'd made it to Heaven or was deep in the slums of Hell. "My baby boy," she howled again. She then gestured towards the door as if to tell the two detectives to escort themselves out. With no hesitation the two detectives found their way out, leaving their barely-drank cups on the mail table beside the front door.

"Sorry for your loss," O'Massey yelled, with almost a snicker, as Wolfe slammed the door behind him.

Ms. Rhodes fell over beside herself. Tears rolling from her eyes like steam trains—the grief of losing her son taking over her...

…

Wolfe and O'Massey sped out of the hellhole they thought of Noble back to the station. "Fucking inbreeds," shouted Shane, "Not one damn person in that town ain't of the same gene pool!"

"Shut the fuck up, Shane," Wolfe insisted.

After a fifteen minute or so drive, Wolfe pulled his car back in front of the station. As he got out, he looked over his shoulder, as if he expected someone was watching him. Shane, being as observant as a blind sloth, did not notice his boss's paranoia; he walked into the station. Wolfe scanned the trees and bushes crowding around the station. Homeless and laborers alike walked around the station, on their way to work, or on their way to spend their last meal ticket on a hit, either way he didn't care, he felt something...*looming* over him. "Shit," he grumbled under his breath.

He walked into the station, cursing to himself. Making his way back to his floor, he walked out of the elevator to find Shane standing over Buck's desk.

"Take a look at this," Shane waved him over.

Wolfe walked over to him and looked down on the desk, "Oh, son of a bitch," he exclaimed.

On the desk staring back at him he found the police badge Buck had sworn an oath to for forty or more years of his life, next to a note which read the following: *"I resign."*

7
Old Photos

Allaura rolled over in her twin sized bed, naked, hair a mess. Her alarm was sound asleep, not scheduled to go off for another hour or so. The sound of her phone ringing buzzed her awake. Usually, if it was that early in the day while she was off schedule, the fire department needed her to come in and cover a shift; she was hesitant to answer. Through the squint of her tired eyes she read the Caller ID: Marg.

She answered the call, "Yeah?" The grogginess in her voice added to her usual rasp.

"Jesse's dead," said the woman over the phone through a shockwave of tears.

Allaura's tiredness left her. She shot to the side of the bed looking out the window. The sun wasn't even shining. Her eyes nearly popped from their sockets at the hearing of the news, "What happened," her voice cracked, her free hand covering her mouth.

Ms. Rhodes explained most of what detectives Harrison Wolfe and Shane O'Massey told her. "I could hardly believe it," mourned Margie, "they said he wanted to go down there—he was adamant on it--I just don't see my boy putting himself in danger that'a way."

"Who told you this?" Allaura asked quickly, her head tilting downward, in her gut she already knew whose foul words Ms. Rhodes was regurgitating.

"A man named Wolfe," Margie replied, "and then some other fatass was with him but he didn't say anything."

In Allaura's heart of hearts, she knew something was fishy. They both knew Jesse quite well, they knew deep down all he ever wanted was to find out who burned all his friends alive in that church building. Everything else to him came seconded: relationships, family, a quality life. He wouldn't put himself in harm's way for anything else. It also ate at her that that same man ruled her father's death a "self-conflicted" one after all the evidence she'd given to deem it otherwise.

"Is there anything I can do," Allaura asked, a grit in her voice.

"Well, I need someone to go down to that apartment and grab his things. Not all of it just the important stuff," she replied through sighs and whimpers, "I have a spare key that I made him give me."

"Give me some time," Allaura walked around her bed into her bathroom, "I'll get ready and be over there."

"...Thank you," Margie cried, sniffling.

"I'm gonna let you go, now," Allaura warned, "I'll see you in a bit."

"Okay," Margie replied in a whisper.

Allaura ended the call, slamming the phone face down on the sink. She glanced at herself in the mirror, thoughts of her late father dancing in her head.

She rushed to get ready, throwing on whatever clothes she could. On top of everything she put a hoodie over to cover her arms. Allaura raced out the door making sure to stay quiet as to not wake her brothers and mother.

As the sun fully rose over the prairie, its light was oppressed by the cluster of gray and white puffs in the sky. The west wind moved the clouds to their will. The air was thick and warm with a slight breeze making the leaves dance and echoing the birds' song.

Allaura hated the wind on her bare skin. It brought her nothing but discomfort. She put her hood over her head as she unlocked the door to her burgundy sedan.

That morning drive from Norman south to Noble felt like nothing. Her head was numb with thoughts of her father, that scummy detective, and her now late ex-boyfriend who'd she'd spent most of her growing-up-days with. She couldn't imagine the pain his mother was going through. She'd known the loss of a father, but little could she comprehend the immense pain of losing a child. She felt helpless as she pulled up to the house.

Ms. Rhodes met Allaura at the door, key in hand. Her eyes were watery and seeing the pain illustrated across the poor mother's face brought Allaura to tears. Ms. Rhodes held out the key but Allaura stepped passed her extended hand and grabbed the woman in for a long hug. Marg cried into Allaura's ear, she trembled and shook.

The wind settled, the clouds stood, halted. Allaura led Marg into her house and sat her back on the couch. She took the key from her, but stayed by her side giving her a shoulder to weep on. Allaura, herself, couldn't comprehend it. Someone, even after the tough times, she still admired, was gone. She'd known the pain he'd been dealt throughout his life, the trouble he'd seen—the trouble they'd endured together. Her comforting thought was seeing him high above the clouds in a lawn chair, a drink in his hand. Not a worry in this world or the next, just completely still, drinking his drink, doing absolutely nothing. Finally, the young detective at peace.

Allaura didn't leave until a bit before noon. Marg had cried most of her tears away, for now, but the pain was still great within her. Allaura got back in her car, a gold key in her hoodie pocket, and drove back up to the southside of Norman just along the highway. A stretch of apartment complexes, most abandoned or occupied by squatters, resided there. She pulled up to his, former, building and proceeded up to the third story.

She made it to the top of the stairwell, just feet away from apartment three-three-six. Allaura froze in her tracks, her eyes bugged as she pulled the key from her pocket to realize the knob had been broken off the door. The wind taunted her, cracking open then closing the door again. Fear shot up her spine, but she was no fool, her father taught her to always be prepared.

Allaura lightly made her way back the three flights of stairs making sure her feet didn't alarm of her presence. She made her way to the passenger's side door and reached into her glove compartment for her dad's old service pistol he'd trained her how to use since she was thirteen.

Gun pointed to the floor, she danced back up the steps inching her way back towards the apartment unit. Fear entered her mind's eye, but she refused to succumb to it. She pressed open the door and pointed the gun inside. The living room was clear of intruders. She observed the area, everything was sprung everywhere. Couches thrown over, the fridge emptied and laying on the kitchen floor, the television smashed and thrown—the place was a mess.

"Son of a fucking bitch," Allaura exclaimed.

Gun out, she made her way into the back room. Jesse's bedroom was in the same state as the living and dining room, trashed and vandalized. She proceeded towards his bathroom, stepping over trash and ripped pillows. Not a person in sight, whoever trashed the place was long gone.

Allaura stared down at the room. The sight frightened her. On the back wall, by the bathroom door was Jesse's desk, facing the window. The desk was like the rest of the apartment: trashed, things thrown about any which way. Above all the trash, a note was placed on top. She picked it up, it was an empty envelope but had one word written in red ink: "Dig".

"What the hell..." Allaura muttered under her breath, placing the envelope back in its place.

"Sorry for the mess," A droll voice sounded behind her.

Allaura rose the gun and turned around in a panic. Her eyes raging, finger on the trigger, she was ready to fire. Jesse fell back on the mirror behind him. He quickly drew his weapon from his shoulder holster.

"Relax," he said from across the room.

A heap of emotion overwhelmed Allaura at the sight of his face not sticking out of an open casket. "You--what—what the hell, man?"

Allaura didn't let him answer. She lowered her pistol and cocked the chamber; a bullet flew from the opening, her caught it mid-air. With no hesitation, she threw the bullet at Rhodes' head. He bent over to duck; the bullet hit the mirror behind him so hard it shattered the glass.

"They said you were dead, you ass!"

"It was a pretty good guess," said Jesse with a bit of a smirk.

Allaura stuffed the gun in her waistband, snug behind her back. She stomped forward and slapped Jesse across the chest. He didn't react; the vest took most of the impact just like it took the bullet which was still lodged in the back.

"Your mother is absolutely devastated," Allaura cried, "you need to go tell her you're--"

"They talked to my mom?" With a grog in his voice, Jesse grimaced.

"She's the one who told me," She replied, "She wanted me to collect all the important stuff, but I wouldn't be able to find any of it—look at the state of this place! Who trashed your apartment?"

Jesse began to walk back into the living room. He looked back over his shoulder, I thought you did," he said, "you saw the letter on the desk? It was left here for me after I got back from the double murder on Beaumont."

"I heard about that," Allaura shouted out following him into the living room, "We knew them. They...they were in the fire."

"Yeah," Jesse replied. "Something's going on here, Allaura. I don't know what. But Wolfe is behind it."

Jesse started rummaging through clothes that were strung about. He had a backpack thrown about in the living room. Whatever scraps of clothes, shoes, and necessities he saw, he stuffed into the bag.

"What're you going to do, Jesse?" she asked with a shaky voice.

"You'll see," Jesse smirked, looking up at his ex like she was no more to him than old bathwater, "You know, for a second there, I thought that story you told me about your dad was just your druggie head trying to justify him off-ing himself. But then I arrived at that little house on Beaumont, and I saw the exact same scene you'd described. Two hung girls—clear inconsistencies about the scene—yet, written off as 'self-conflicted' and brushed under the rug...all the same. 'Only difference: these girls appeared to have left notes. Except it wasn't notes at all, it was just an envelope. Bastard can't even afford paper."

Allaura's brow turned pale as the expression on her face sunk to her chest. Her gut sank making her feel the need to puke, "Y-you looked into Dad's death?"

"Somewhat," replied Jesse, "it struck my curiosity. I wasn't about to try and re-open that case. But now it has some relevance. Wolfe is hiding something and I'm going to find out what."

"Do you think Wolfe did it?" Allaura folded her arms within herself, picking at her cuticles.

"...I don't know, he's definitely up to something," Jesse zipped up the backpack and slung it over his right shoulder. The swift movement sent a shockwave through his back. "Gah," he called out, wincing.

"You're hurt," Allaura pointed out.

Jesse turned his back to her and removed his peacoat showing off his bloodied shirt and ripped clothes, "This didn't feel too good," he winced.

"Oh my god!" Allaura cried out covering her mouth and stepping back, her eyes locked on the bullet. "You should be dead..."

"No, sadly," Jesse sighed, looking down at his trashed floor, "I'm alive for a reason. I should be dead; most days I wish I was dead...but I am alive...for a purpose. Or maybe just a bad joke I'm still alive"

Allaura stood there in silence for a moment. She felt her shoulders tense up and her insides start to tremble. She'd known parts of the young detective she wishes she hadn't and knowing that he wasn't overexaggerating when he talked about death made her heart ill. She stepped closer to him with hesitance, "You need to go see her mother," she reminded him, "she's heartbroken."

"I can't," Jesse replied, "they'll be watching her house. If I get seen and they figure out I'm alive they'll try and kill me again, I'm sure. I need to let them live blissfully while I move around in the shadows, until I can uncover what they've been trying to hide."

"They're holding a memorial service for you," Allaura said, "Tuesday morning."

"Good. Go to it with Mama," Jesse opened the door and stepped out of his apartment, "If I need you, I'll call you. Flip over my mattress, I think there are some old photos in there for her. Hopefully the frames aren't broken."

As he walked out, she stayed staring at the open door, hearing his footsteps clammer down each step. With a sigh, she went back into the bedroom and lifted the mattress back onto the box spring. A cluster of pictures in various-sized frames were scattered about. She picked up two in one hand. She flipped over the frames to see a picture of the young detective among a large group of kids his age, standing right next to Allaura. All of them were smiling, including Jesse. She remembered the picture; it was taken when they all went to church. It pained her to look at it, even for a moment, knowing that nearly everyone in that picture had died. including the two girls that were found dead two nights ago on Beaumont Street.

Allaura was unsettled staring at the old photo for merely a few seconds. Jesse stared at that picture every single day to remind himself why he lived on. Norman may have forgotten the tragedy that happened at that church that night, but Jesse refused to forget.

Allaura collected more of the pictures and hurried out of the apartment...

8

Black Leather

Grey clouds descended from the sky and mingled with the trees that eerie Tuesday morning. As the cities and towns that were left ruled under Common Law heard of the devastation down south, they gathered there in front of the station to honor the fallen: Detective Jesse David Rhodes.

The press gathered as well as high-ranking officers, his fellow detectives, and the rest of the Norman Police Department. Ms. Margie Rhodes sat front row along with Allaura who held her hand as the poor mother in black rose a handkerchief to her tearful eyes. Jesse hadn't gone to tell his mother the good news: he didn't die. Allaura knew he hadn't, but she comforted his mother every day since with thoughts of beating his ass sideways as she did it.

On stage Head Detective Harrison Wolfe, Shane O'Massey, and the higher-ranked officers congregated waiting for the ceremony to begin. The right-hand corner of the stage a framed picture of the fallen detective stood on an aisle with red roses placed at the feet.

Detective Wolfe was set to give a few kind words. In his hand, as he approached the microphone, was a fistful of note cards.

"Let us begin in prayer," said Wolfe, the crowd collectively bowing their heads. "Dear, Lord, we gather in your presence today..."

Wolfe dragged on the prayer; as very head bowed in reverence to the God above, The Young Detective Jesse Rhodes lurked around the throng making sure his steps were mute.

He wore a black hoodie matched with black jeans with his peacoat thrown over top of it. To hide his face, he wore a black bandana across his nose and mouth. Allaura unbowed her head and looked across the crowd of seated prayers to notice him attempting to circle the building. Jesse caught glimpse of her gaze, he pointed to Wolfe on the stage as if to say: "Don't look at me!" Allaura rolled her eyes and proceeded to bow her head again.

"...In God's name we pray, amen," continued Wolfe.

By the time the collective audience rose their heads, Jesse was to the side of the stage. His hands folded in his coat pockets, just looking at the man who'd presumed him dead.

"Jesse Rhodes dedicated his young life to giving back to his community," he began, "all he ever wanted to do was help others,"

Just the opening sentence left a bitter taste in the young detective's mouth. That wasn't his intentions at all, he just wanted to find out who burned his friends alive. Even though how harsh it may sound, he couldn't care less for the community of Norman, Oklahoma. What had they ever done for him that had him feel the need to *give back* to?

"All this young man ever wanted was to be a shining light to those around him. I can surely say, he's left quite the impression on me."

As if in perfect sync, Jesse and Allaura rolled their eyes. The more he spoke the more Jesse wanted to throw up and the more Allaura begged the question: "Have you ever met this selfish bastard?"

The crowd gathered, a bit more than a hundred in attendance, mostly members of the press, gave sorrowful, longing looks to the man on stage. Word had spread like tornado debris about the young detective's disappearance while working on a case in Pauls Valley. Press then drew their attention back to Goodman and the similar circumstances of his disappearance. Safe to say, Norman as well as the rest of the state was hooked at what the hell was going on ten miles south of the capital.

From the glimpses of Rhodes' face and pictures of him and his family that had been playing on the news and printed in every newspaper everyone, the town couldn't help but feel remorse. They painted Rhodes as a blue-collar family-man who cared about nothing more than his community. A man who took pride in serving his for those around him. A true-blue-ribbon hero.

Some in the crowd wiped their tears away with the black silks they wore in respect. The more the dead man, alive, looked on the more the rage in his belly roared. Jesse couldn't play his aces too quickly. The longer they thought he was dead the more time he had to lurk in the shadows and discover the secrets only he alone could reveal.

"...Jesse grew up here his entire life. The love he had for his community; how driven he was to make this piece of Earth a better place in such desperate times... it's something only myself could aspire to achieve..." Wolfe drew a long pause, eyeing the crowd. In the silence the rush of the wind echoed through the microphone. Grayer clouds rolled in clashing with the fog. The morning was so dark it looked more like sundown.

As Harrison Wolfe drooled on longer, Jesse had enough listening. He glanced at the front row; his mother was holding it together, hardly. He felt a glimpse of agony for her. With that last glance, the young detective fell back into a crowd of onlookers and retreated to the right side of the building.

Along that brick wall was the fire escape expanding from the second story all the way up to the roof. He jumped up gripping the ladder, it falling down with him. He marched up the steps then scaling each one of the floor's escapes until he made it all the way to the roof. Jesse rolled over the railing and made his way to the north entrance. He couldn't help but peer over the side looking down on everyone for a second.

Jesse used the roof as an escape. He spent most of his workdays up there just to have a brief moment of solitude. The door to access the roof only had a knob on the inside. So he wouldn't lock himself out, he stuffed a rag between the door hinge and the metal frame so it would never close all the way.

He swung the door open feeling the draft of a week's worth of Oklahoma weather escaping the stairwell. It was a cold breeze, then a heatwave, then a foggy humidity. like all the bipolar weather the state had to offer found a hip, new place to mingle.

With a multitude of coughs, Jesse raced down the stairwell until he reached the entrance to his department floor.

The floor, much like the rest of the building, was deprived of people. They were all out paying respects to the Dead Detective. It was the perfect opportunity for Jesse to be sneaking around.

He didn't know what he was looking for or what he would find. The feeling of uncertainty uneased his nerves. His steps fell lightly tapping the wooden floor, not making a sound. As if anyone would hear him. The sound of Wolfe's words oozed through the walls in a muffled hum. Jesse couldn't make out any of the words; that didn't bother him a bit. He made his way towards the array of desks in the center of the room—Buck's O'Massey's and Goodman's which later became occupied by late Detective Rhodes.

At first glance Jesse notice the badge displayed on Buck's. The note placed under it in full view gave more than an explanation. *Seems sudden,* Jesse thought.

His read on Buck made him feel the man was more sympathetic than anything else. He was more God-fearing than the rest of the detectives. At one point in his life, which he told the Young Detective, Buck was a pastor of a church down in Lexington. He believed in the Good Lord wholeheartedly. He proclaimed, multiple times, joining the force was what God told him to do. Buck proclaimed God said he would "die a detective.

Jesse lightly picked up the badge, w*hy would a God-fearing man suddenly go against his will?*

He suddenly remembered the last time he saw Buck. The former pastor was pleading with Wolfe to not send Jesse down to Pauls Valley. *Why would he care either way? Unless he knew something I didn't...*

The Young Detective stifled through Buck's drawers—emptied and bare. Nothing left except cobwebs and dust. Slamming the doors shut, Jesse peered over the desk staring across the room at the door to Wolfe's office. He knew if he'd find anymore answers, and not more questions...they'd be in there.

Slowly, Jesse cracked open the door. A scowl smeared across his face as the light from the room glistened his face. The lights were off; candles burned atop the desk. Flicking on the light, he circled the desk. Everything looked in place—the room an array of organized clutter from the walls to the desk.

He stifled through the top drawers on each side of the desk. In the left was all of Wolfe 's main, opened and unopen, scattered about mindlessly. In the right, clutter and keepsakes like lighters and batteries as well as pocketknives, scrap paper, and old pens. Nothing of any use, he slammed the drawer back with frustration. He then paraded through the bottom drawers on the right finding more useless junk.

With authority, he yanked open the bottom right drawer--completely empty. Just a plank of wood with a small hole near the bottom looking back at him. His temple and fists clinched as he hunched over the voided compartment. A swear nearly escaped his lips but he wouldn't allow it to fall out in case ears were listening. His face grew redder and redder with aggravation. Then it hit him. The small hole at the base of the plank...not much more than the tip of a pen could fit in there. As a last act of desperation, Jesse reached into one of the junk drawers to retrieve an ink pen. With caution, he stuck the pen tip through the small hole...

With a click the false bottom unhinged from the mechanism holding it in place. Like a rushing breeze relief flushed over the Young Detective. He reached in and grabbed the plank of wood and placed it on the desktop. Staring back at him: a black leather satchel with a brown cloth strap.

This is it, Jesse's mind raced, *this should have some answers.*

He picked it up brought it out into the open. Standing up, he slapped it on the desk turning over the flap. Without hesitation Jesse ripped out the contents of the satchel. It was an array of pictures. There was six in total. Jesse scattered them across the desk.

Each picture was of six different houses. Some angles were from a street view, some from up close peering through a window, something had leaves blurred close to the lens indicating they were taken from in a tree or behind a bush. They were all taken in different times of day. Some in the morning, some in the blanket of night. But all had one common connection: a woman—the same woman appeared in each photograph. Clearly, she was unaware of the pictures being taken, or of the photographer taking them. In the stills, she's participating in regular homely activities: cooking, cleaning, roaming through the house; nothing scandalous about any of them.

The woman herself was of fair build. She was older, maybe around Wolfe's age, but she seemed to take good care of herself. She had short silver hair and thin glasses; she dressed rather expensive. Jewelry crowded her fingers and pearls looped her neck like a python.

Jesse didn't recognize the woman at all. And more so he didn't know why these stills would be hidden in the false bottom of Wolfe's desk.

Jesse looked in the black satchel again. The main compartment was void like the drawer it came in. Jesse turned the bag upside down and shook it with aggression and vigor. Something metal rattled inside, it quickly fell out and bounced around on the desk. Rattling across the desk: a silver-plated key.

He picked up the key and observed it close to his eyes. There wasn't a save in the room. Nothing with a keyhole. Unless a picture frame hid one somewhere in the room. But before the Young Detective had time to overturn every picture, his phone began to buzz in his pocket.

"Talk to me," he picked up the phone.

"The service just ended, Wolfe went back into the building," Allaura's voice sounded frantic.

Jesse's eyes darted at the door. He could hear footsteps, faint down the corridor. Quickly he crammed the pictures back into the black leather satchel and forced it back into the false bottom. Rushed, sweat dripping from his brow, he hurried to make the desk look exactly as he found it.

He hung the phone up without a formal goodbye and shoved the phone as well as the key into the inside pocket of his peacoat.

Epiphany struck him, maybe the key didn't belong to something in the office, rather, at his house. Jesse ripped open the mail drawer once again, looking through addresses. He disregarded ones that were sent to the office address. After rummaging through a handful of mail, he found a home address: 601 12th Ave, Norman.

Jesse crammed the letter into his pocket and headed for the door, but he was stopped in his tracks. He could hear the muffled voices of Head Detective Harrison Wolfe and Detective Shane O'Massey. His heart sank to his gut.

He had to act quick; footsteps drew nearer. Jesse peered towards the window to his left. With haste he unlocked the hinges and slid the window up. A gust of wind entered the room as Jesse threw his body out the window landing on a fire escape. Just a second before Wolfe swung the door to his office wide open, Jesse slammed the window closed from the outside and fled down the fire escape.

The Young Detective left the NPD building how he did not intend to: with more answers than questions. But, deep down, he knew he was one step closer.

9
Consider the Lillies, Mr. Wolfe

It'd been a week and a half since the memorial service. The shadows were where Rhodes called home. The homeless dens across town, in his car, the homeless shelter on Porter. Daytime was when the young detective laid his head to rest. All while the key and the home address of Head Detective Harrison Wolfe dwindled in his pocket.

Jesse knew he needed to be swift with every action. He couldn't spare acting on impulse and ruining his best chance at cracking the mystery wide open. He owed it to himself just like he owed it to those girls on Beaumont Street. Like he owed it to Goodman. Like he owed it to Norman.

The Young Detective kept a keen eye on all the players in the game. Just before the labor bell would ring off at five 'o' clock, he'd steak out Wolfe's car in front of the Norman Police Department building. Watching as that slimy Wolfe and that putrid O'Massey would slither to their cars and retreat to their holes in the mud. Once Wolfe was a good distance away, Rhodes would tail him.

Wolfe would never go straight home. From five to roughly past midnight, Wolfe would frequent one of the local clubs on Campus Corner. The one Rhodes knew all too well: The Pit.

If you knew anything about anything in this town, or even if you didn't, you knew for a fact The Pit was a hub for drugs and prostitution. Whores and druggies danced step-for-step on their decent to Hell. All while the

Young Detective watched from the shadows as an old man in the corner sipped his drink.

No one ever came to meet Wolfe, Rhodes noticed. Not a friend, a lover, or an escort to keep him company. He just sat there for hours. He ordered the same thing every night: Irish Whiskey, straight.

The club, let alone the entire Corner, was packed with people. If Wolfe were to ever see him, it be because Rhodes allowed him to. But Jesse was still young, all he needed was a striped t-shirt and tight-fitting jeans and he'd fit right in. Which is exactly what he did. To add to the moniker of a basic young person, he'd apply dark mascara across his eyes to delude his face to anyone who might've seen his memorial on the news.

Like it was clockwork, night-after-night, Wolfe showed up at the club at five and left just past midnight. After four nights of this, Jesse grew curiouser and curiouser, and a tad cocky. As the bar was jammed full of people, Jesse reached the attention of one of the bar maids working the floor.

"Hey," he said deepening his voice, "what's that guy in the corner doing?"

"That guy?" She turned around and looked at the man, "He's here every night; he's harmless. Just sits there with his whiskey."

"Does he ever meet anyone?"

"I wouldn't know," she replied, "I can't really say."

Rhodes got closer to the woman's ear. "Look." he said awkwardly, "he's my dad. My mom asked me to come here. I know it's kind of idiotic, but she's worried he's seeing other women. So, has he seen anyone?"

The bartender thought for a moment, sympathizing with Rhodes, "Well, to be completely honest, I've seen him meet with only one person before. But it wasn't a woman. In fact, yeah, yeah, yeah, I remember. This real creepy-looking guy. Had a bunch of scars on his face. He wore a COVID-mask, so I didn't see all his face. His eye was just real fucked up."

A man with a fucked-up eye? Rhodes was taken back by this. "Did you catch a name?"

"I didn't. You don't really catch names in a place like this. But I am curious to catch whatever you got," she smiled and fluttered her eyes.

Jesse paused for a moment, getting lost in his gaze at Wolfe, a bit of him fuming. Ignoring her advances, he slipped the woman a twenty-dollar bill, "Get him another round. Keep the change."

"Uh--'kay then," she said. The woman walked behind the bar, poured the whiskey in the glass and presented it to Wolfe. He looked confused for a moment, she placed it on the table and continued on. From then onto the rest of the night, Wolfe didn't touch that glass of whiskey. Then, again, just past midnight, he left the club.

…

For the first time in weeks the clouds cleared and the sun beat down. The air was thick with heat, almost unbearable. Like the last day, the day before, and the day before that, Detective Rhodes staked out the Norman PD Building.

His motor hummed as he stared at the fuel meter. It read just below a quarter of a tank. Gas was pricey and scarce. Money was little to come by, especially since Jesse was no longer on the payroll and whatever money he had yet to collect went to his mother. He lived off peanuts and table scraps, but it was all with purpose. He knew it was time to act.

Wolfe's car was parked in front like it was every day. Jesse rattled his engine and persisted down the road to 1701 Gray Street.

It was no more than a five-minute drive from the station. Jesse pulled up to the two-story house in that quiet neighborhood. The brightness of the sun was blocked out by the thick trees that lined the sidewalks. Luckily for Jesse, each house had a line of trees between each property line—his sneaking around wouldn't be seen so easily.

A brown SUV was parked in the driveway as Jesse pulled up to the curb. With a mask over his face and a hood over his head, he approached the house. Nearly tiptoeing, he past the SUV peering inside for a moment before stepping onto the porch.

To the left of the welcome mat was a porch swing and a window with a metal cage around it. The wood the porch was built was unkept, chipping away at itself and faded by the elements.

Jesse was more than prepared to bust in with force. To be thorough, he checked under the "welcome" mat. To his luck he found a spare key.

With ease he unlocked the door and proceeded into the house. Staring into Wolfe's living room, must like his office, were picture frames hanging about every inch of the wall. He closed the door slowly behind him. Among the vast amount of pictures, rifles, handguns and shotguns had their fair share of space on the walls. Above the living room was a balcony attached to a flight of stairs.

The wooden floor creaked with every footstep the Young Detective took. Up the stairs he went, the wood creaking under his feet. When he made it to the top Jesse grazed his face around the corner—no one was down the hall. The house was hush. Despite the car in the driveway, Jesse safely assumed the house was void and Wolfe was most likely too head-deep in paperwork to intrude.

The upstairs was lined with doors on both sides of the wall. The first three doors he opened were empty rooms with well-kept beds. The fourth: Wolfe's office. Much like his at work, it was lined with pictures from wall-to-window-to-wall. Jesse never took the time to observe them, he didn't care about this man's personal life. As he walked through the door, it clicked in his mind that maybe his personal life held relevance. He stared at each one taking in their stills of information.

The ones framed on his desk gave the Young Detective more insight than the ones on the wall. He picked up the gray frame, confused.

Wolfe dressed in black, and a lover coated in white along with a Tribal Chief in a long-flowing head dress between them. Wolfe looked much younger, as did his bride who he swore he'd seen before.

The black frame: Wolfe and his bride, much older, with three young adults smiling with them at the camera; two boys, one girl. The image took him by surprise. The woman. The woman in the eerie stills sitting in the false bottom of Wolfe's work desk...it's his wife.

Rhodes placed the pictures back on the desk. Throwing caution to the wind, he threw open the drawers looking for more answers. Through his things Jesse stifled through like looking for thread amongst twine. But, in the rummage, he found no more than old pens and open letters.

After going through all the drawers and removing their miscellaneous contents to check for false bottoms. To his dismay there were none.

For a moment the Young Detective thought, his mind's eye looming in its own realm. *This isn't his office,* his mind spoke, *he has no reason to be sneaky. Whatever it is I'm looking for, it's out in the open.*

Like a god sniffing the dirt for a buried bone, Jesse followed his senses to the next room across the hall to the far left—the master bedroom, as it were.

The bed, like the others, well made, unbothered. The floor and rug were well-kept like a showpiece. To him, it seemed like no one had lived there in a while. Despite the car out from which indicated someone was in the house with him, yet nothing but Jesse's own shadow fueled his paranoia.

Unlike the rest of the house, shrouded with picture frames of old memories, the master room had only one picture dangling to the right of the bed. It hung from face-level and was around three-feet wide.

With a tiptoe in his step, he crept to it, still not aware if someone else lingered in the house with him. The picture was a pastel painting locked within a golden frame. With caution overwhelming his belly, the Young Detective lifted the frame from its hanger and moved it to the bed hoping that underneath would be a safe of some sorts. And to his luck, he found exactly what he'd hoped for.

The safe imbedded in the wall was the same height and length as the fame which shielded it. Absent of a combination lock, a keyhole rested in its place.

Without a moment to waste Jesse Rhodes fumbled the key from his pocket, hoping for a match. The key slid in with ease like butter across bread. After a elongated, anxious breath, he applied the pressure needed to turn the key to unlock the safe. As if the heavens aligned perfectly with the stars, the key turned and the mechanisms within jolted free.

Jesse, shrills through his spine, opened the safe as wide as he could swing the door back on its hinges. Within the safe itself, the Jesse Rhodes, a man dead to the world, a Phantom on the Prairie, saw exactly the thing he'd hoped to find: a case file box.

Answers, Jesse thought. With no hesitation, he ripped the box from the sacred cubby. The weight of the box was paramount, contrary its size. He threw the box atop the bed disregarding the painting.

Jesse threw away the lid as quick as he could. Like a hunger, he needed to see which Wolfe kept so secluse. Not even to be kept safe within the Norman Police Department Headquarters.

At first Jesse thought of The Church Fire—the case left unsolved in which the Young Detective dedicated his life to on the chance of solving for his community. *It must be,* he thought, *it has to be.*

A file laid on top of a plethora of more files. His hands began to clinch as he reached for the file which set atop. The feeling in his gut did not lay to rest. Opening it felt as if it were to only happen in his dreams. But what he succeeded to discover was not what he'd intended at all.

Within that first file staring back at him were the photos taken of the two girls on Beaumont Steet, Lola Everett and Elisabeth York.

The remembrance of their hanging bodies struck him ill. He flipped the photos in the file like a book, reading, studying. At the back end of the file, Jesse bared witnessed to a slip of paper written in red ink. The words written: "5 & 6 of 37".

The breath in his lungs vanished like vapor. The note caught him by surprise. It was the same handwriting as the note which he found in his trashed apartment. After he studied it for a moment, he turned it over like a page and examined the next piece of evidence: the note which Jesse bared witness to at the crime scene itself; the envelope which read "Acknowledge me".

Jesse turned over the envelope noting the first time he'd seen it, it was void—not this time. Turning over the flap, a letter laid within it; a crumbled piece of paper folded neatly.

Wolfe told Jesse before he sent him to Pauls Valley that they'd found the girls' suicide letters under the bed after he'd left. The Young Detective ripped out the letter and unfolded it so he may read their last words:

Consider the lilies, Mr. Wolfe. So gentle and delicate. Just like these two girls, Mr. Wolfe. You've been doing a splendid job covering up my filth for me, I thank you for that. You're truly doing the devil's work while I carry out the acts of my God. I do wish I could communicate with you person-to-person, but frankly I don't wish to compromise my task at hand to seek you out. Keep at Logies. When I need to communicate with you, I will. Always be prepared. The Kingdom is at hand.

--Disciple

"What the hell," Rhodes murmured, his breath catching in his throat.

Jesse placed the letter back in the file and proceeded to pull the next one from the pile. His hands shook, his brow sweated as he peered open the file to see another victim hung by the neck. Behind the pictures he found yet another note: "4 of 37". Jesse lurked within the file some more; studying the male in the picture. He'd recognized him like he did the two girls. He was a burn victim, just like them as well. His face and neck, as well as his arms and back were deformed from the burns.

"Harold Smith", the file read. "Hung by the neck", Ruled: Suicide. Date: May 11, last year.

No additional note was attached inside the file. Jesse moved onto the next one. "3 of 37". Rhodes nearly dropped the folder as he looked down upon the crime scene photos of Brent Ellis hanging from his ceiling fan. As be observed the photos, he noticed the safe was wide open and empty just like Allaura had described to him.

Behind the photos, he found a note. Upon the envelope in red: "Acknowledge me" and inside the letter it read:

I do the lord's bidding, Mr. Wolfe. But today, I have sinned. He wasn't a part of the plan God bestowed upon my natural body, but I couldn't help myself. The rage, the anger, the folly all built up inside me for years on end. I hate him. In my repentance, I'll sacrifice a goat. I'll leave it on university grounds, perhaps you'll read of it in the paper.

Mr. Wolfe, sir. I do not wish you to be angry with me. You are but a mortal man. The inner workings of God's will be too complex for a man not of the faith to understand. So that is why I must motivate you in the manner in which I do. It's not personal, only by God's hand do my actions follow. Never forget that.

Allow me to be clear: I will have no remorse against your wife if you are to alert anyone of my doings. She will be brutalized, maimed, deformed, beaten. Her only comfort will be the death she slowly succumbs to, eventually. Remember this, Mr. Wolfe. I will not stop until all thirty-seven are finished. My next contact will be at our same spot. It'll be some time but remember, if I don't see you there when I arrive, I will kill your wife. If I am found out in any way, I will kill your wife. If you defy me, guess what...I WILL KILL YOUR WIFE.

Sorry to be crass. You must understand my situation. God is counting on me to finish the work he started. I do not intend on failing him. It would've been easier if you cared about your detectives a bit more, I wouldn't have to go to these lengths.

That night God meant to rid of all those children in that church. He rained down his hellfire like Sodom and Gomorrah upon those unclean spirits. He did good. He got most of them, but the thirty-four that remain he's left up to me. Like King Baldwin IV of Jerusalem, The Leper King, I will charge my weakened body into battle and avenge my God and all who serve him.

God's will has just begun.

Jesse dropped the file in his hands and stumbled back. His fright of the severity of what was going on overwhelmed Rhodes. Suddenly, it all started to make sense. Norman had a serial killer on its hands.

10

The Pawns and the Player

Wolfe's Log:

Today I was remembering the time my wife and I decided on Norman. We were fresh from campus with our degrees; the world was ours to claim. We could've gone anywhere in the world. I wanted to try California. Sunny beaches and swimming pools. I always wanted that life. But my love, well, she wanted family and family was and has always been Oklahoma. What was I to do? Her eyes were my smile, her beauty: my eyes begged to see, and her love was the very air I breathe. If she rooted in the plains, I'd root deeper!

I think on that wishing I'd egged her differently. I should've told her this shithole was exactly what it is, and we are to abandon it immediately. But I didn't. I didn't for love. And it made her so, so happy.

But now I see that I have doomed her and I. It was a slow-ticking clock on a raggedy, old wall. But soon enough, the howled on its last hour.

Tshallah. Retore myself. Restore my family. Save us. Redeem us. I waited on the Lord my whole life. And I kept waiting. And I waited more. And, yet, in my old age I still cry out to you...waiting, still. I hate you. I just want my wife back.

End log.

Rhodes folded the letter and put it away. He sat on the edge of Wolfe's bed and buried his head in his palms. A picture on the wall caught his eye: Wolfe, dead pan; another news article about him. He noted how the old Wolfe's cheeks drooped and his eyes slummed down with heavy bags. Rhodes felt that same expression washing over him. The look of gravity plummeting down the situation—it all finally made sense. But Rhodes looked for the blissful ignorance that was apparent just moments ago.

Jesse held true to the old Wolfe's sentiment: *I hate you.* First the church fire, then Allaura, then the Beaumont murders, then Pauls Valley...now a serial killer. A serial killer with a personal liking to the church fire. Rhodes was sure God was entertained. He's sure the popcorn was well-buttered and ready to munch while observing the events that were about to transpire. Rhodes could've run. He could've put the box back where he'd found it, drove to his mother and drove as far as far goes. But that would've been easy. And Rhodes never knew what easy meant.

The young detective piled the evidence into his vehicle and sped off. He had to make a pit stop before the war was set in motion.

South only ever went as far as Noble for Rhodes. For the first time in months, the bad son, finally went to go see his mother. But not in good spirits.

The gray clouds over the Dragoons March solidified the day. Rhodes was too proud to walk in. He knocked, then when that didn't work, he rang the doorbell.

"MOM?" Rhodes' voice cracked and the frog hopped in his throat.

Silence overtook the Rhodes' residence. Slowly, the woman behind the red door crept her eyes to see the visitor. Her eyes were red while her skin pale. She'd been crying her eyes for her lost son, just for him to be embarrassingly at her doorstep.

The gasp of shock and relief was like a tornado siren going off. She lost hold of the door and fell to her knees. "No--they—oh my God!" she couldn't get a word out. Her breath overtook her.

"Mama," Rhodes grabbed her, dropping down to her, "it's me, Mama. I'm sorry."

She didn't speak a word. She held her boy like she'd never held him before. Like she'd already lost him twice. "Devil keeps tryin' to get you but you just won't go down!" She said through watery tears.

"He should try harder when he tries a third time," Rhodes broke a smile.

With his mother in his hands, he rose to his feet. "Mama," he spoke softly, "You won't understand, but you have to leave."

She saw the serious gaze in the eyes she gave him. Ms. Rhodes wasn't a dumb woman; she knew when something was afoot. "It's about those detectives, isn't it?"

"It's bigger than them," Rhodes said.

"I'll go pack," she said, "Call me when you kill those bastards!"

Within the half hour Ms. Rhodes packed a light back and was on her way. At the car, she grabbed

Rhodes by the jaw, looking him in the eye and said: "Win!" And with that, she drove off.

Rhodes waved her car down the street by the house he grew up in. All the memories flooded him at once. The good, the bad, and the regrettable. Rhodes calmed his nerves and checked his watch: quarter passed five. It was about time for a drink...

The bones in his body jittered to the beat. He carried all the evidence he needed with him in his peacoat. No more sporting the preppy, in-fashion attire like he had been when stalking Wolfe. It was back to the kept suit and peacoat for the young detective. He kept his eyes glazed over on the usual seat that was yet to be occupied.

As night fell more and more came to party. It was so easy to get lost in the dim light and loud music. It was a live concert that night in the club. But Rhodes was there on purpose. The only pleasure there was to be had was when he exposed the old Wolfe.

And like clockwork, there he was. With a black brimmed hat, the drooped-over look on his face, the rain-stained peacoat. Rhodes watched over him like a hawk to a rabbit. Or should I say: A wolf to a sheep.

Wolfe traced his finger around the rim of his drink. His eyes glazed over in thought. Perhaps tonight he'd be visited by *him*, he thought. Little did he know.

Rhodes marched to the table and to the sound of the bass, he slammed the evidence down, the files and papers scattering about, rage filling Jesse's bugged eyes, "You killed me to protect him?"

Wolfe leaned back against the wall behind him. Nearly reaching for his gun until he saw the familiar face. His face drooped lower than usual; his eyes finding it difficult to process the ghost standing before him. "Holy--" he couldn't even finish the line.

"Care to explain?" Rhodes yelled over the music.

Wolfe looked down at the files; with great angst he recognized them. "You've been in my house!" Wolfe retorted, "You son of a bitch!"

"You tried to have me killed!"

Wolfe shot up slamming his hands down nearly cracking the table, "HE'S GOING TO KILL MY WIFE!"

Rhodes and Wolfe stared each other down, their rage topping one another's. Wolfe glanced over Rhodes' left shoulder; his rage turned into shock. Before the young detective could see what had caught his eye, the sound of a hammer being cocked back sounded behind his head.

"I see you've been digging," said a still, calm voice into Rhodes' ear.

Wolfe sat back down with ease in his descend. He kept his hands flat on the table over the scattered stack of files; his eyes locked just beyond Rhodes' left shoulder. Rhodes kept his eyes on Wolfe. The rage in his eyes slowly faded into gumption to survive. He'd done it before; he could do it again.

"I see you've been busy," Rhodes replied, "Did a stellar job covering your tracks."

"Not without the help of our friend, here. Sit down."

Rhodes carefully pulled out the seat below him and made slow work of sitting. Once he was sat, he placed his hands atop the table. The man then made his way around, finding the empty third seat. Rhodes stared him down.

A black jacket and hood along with matching gloves covered most of him. His face was obstructed by the help of a glossy, silver mask. It had no expression on it, just indents for eyeholes and a small slit for the mouth. The skin that showed through the eyeholes was beat red and pale in some parts. But the eyes, oh the eyes, they were as dead as his victims.

The man in the silver mask crept the gun under the table. He periodically switched who he had the gun pointed at, unbeknownst to them. His head was tilted down as he looked at them, observing their displeasure of the situation and finding enjoyment in their anxiety.

"I'm glad we all made it here, tonight. I didn't think things would work out so well."

His voice was very gruff as if he'd been punched in the throat. He may just be trying to deepen it to mask his true voice, Rhodes deduced. With an acute sigh, Rhodes leaned forward, "I take it you're the one who trashed my fucking apartment."

"It could've been worse. I could've trashed your mom's place."

Rhodes' rage shot up from his soul and through his chest. The only thing that brought him relief was knowing she was long gone, up the road, hopefully out of harm's way. "Bastard," Rhodes gritted his teeth, wanting to scream.

"Wolfe... you didn't kill him like I asked you to."

"Where is my wife you son of a bitch?!" Wolfe banged his hands on the table. The aggression in his body couldn't hide the helplessness in his eyes.

The man in the silver mask just stared at Wolfe. You could see through the eye slits the smile marks behind his eyes. He slowly turned his head back to Rhodes, "*Jesse Rhodes. Detective* Jesse Rhodes. That surely has a different ring to it. It's strange when people grow up the titles they take along the way. I never would've guessed."

"We know each other?" Rhodes looked confused.

"No. Never met. But I know of you."

The man leaned in closer. Through the grog in his voice, leaning the tip of the gun on Rhodes' thigh, he whispered, "*I... burned ...you."*

He slowly fell back in his chair as Rhodes felt his heart sink into his lap.

"I kept an eye on everyone from that night. Watching and watching... and watching... waiting. Until my time *festering* was done with. It's time to finish what was started."

"Y-you burned down the church?" Rhodes could only mutter. A tear escaped his eye, his hands started to shake flat on the table.

"Rhodes!" Wolfe shouted.

"You killed my friends?"

The man looked at Rhodes, his smile scars became even more defined, "I'll burn this town down to feel its warmth. You're the lucky one, Jesse. You're going to be last."

Just before Jesse could jump up and avenge everyone he'd ever known, a waitress came by the table, "Drinks, guys?"

You could hear the chuckle escape his silver mask. The man shot up like lightning and aimed the gun at the woman. He shot her like lame mule—through the head. Rhodes and Wolfe jumped startled at the initial shot as the woman fell. The man then jolted for the door shooting wildly in the air. The people in the club hit the ground. The man made it out the door; Wolfe and Rhodes grabbed their guns and badges.

"NORMAN P.D. EVERYONE ON THE GROUND!" Wolfe shouted as the two sprinted out the door.

People on the sidewalk looked startled and confused as the two detectives hurried outside. Rhodes caught eye of someone looking at him, "Which way did he go?!" he yelled.

She pointed down the alleyway next to the club. Wolfe and Rhodes pointed their guns and started down the alleyway. Suddenly, they stopped their advance. The man turned the corner back into the alleyway, revealing himself to them. He had something in his hand...someone in his hand. She was struggling, wincing, screaming, pleading. At first, they thought she was just some random club-goer he'd taken hostage. No, Wolfe recognized her cries.

"KAREY!" Wolfe screamed.

"HARRISO--"

She was silenced by the unforgiving sound of a pistol.

The shriek, the absolute guttural cry Wolfe let out as his wife fell, and his knees gave out under him, would stick inside Rhodes' mind for the years to follow. He'd wake up to the sound of that nasty cry plenty of times a night.

The man paused for a moment. He eyed Rhodes down the alleyway in the darkness between them. Wolfe made it to his feet, weakly, and ran to his wife.

By the time he'd reached her, the man in the silver mask was already gone. And all that was left was a young detective, and a broken wolf.

11

Blood-Stained Suit

Units arrived from all over town. Every oinker in the city didn't know to be more in shock at the sight of Mrs. Wolfe's brutal murder or the sight of the detective whose eulogy they all stood in attendance for. They were smart not to ask questions.

It took two officers to pull Wolfe from his wife. When they managed to finally relief him from the corpse, from his mouth to his pants, he was drenched in red. From the alleyway, where Jesse watched on, his whimpers molested his ears.

Cops passed by the onlooking detective. Forensics finally appeared and started passing in-and-out the door as well—Jesse did not budge. His hands were folded down towards his lap watching those two cops struggle to bring Wolfe out to the ambulance on scene to relief him of some of his shock; again, Jesse just kept looking on.

A sergeant took notice of Jesse; he figured he was just reading the crime scene—that's what he wrote his nonhumanness off to be. Him, being just as dazed and confused by the situation, had to break the silence lurking the home.

"Hey, uh, Rhodes," he said, a shakiness in his voice, "what the hell happened here?"

Jesse took his sweet time to turn his head to glance at the cop. Jesse's dead, unfeeling, eyes stabbed through the gaze of that police sergeant. The stare was so off-putting to him, he took a step back from the detective.

"Call Shane," he finally said, "He's the lead on this one."

With that, Detective Jesse Rhodes unperched from the alley and began walking away from the scene. "Oh," he cried out, turning back to the sergeant, "give him this!" Jesse threw the envelope to him, landing on his chest. The blood that had partially dried on it stuck to his cloth before ripping off and falling to the wooden planks.

Jesse walked off into the night. The Police Headquarters was no more than about a mile or more away. Jesse walked across to eastside of town, which by far was the worst side of town. It was where the "Looney Bin" as the locals called it was. But it's proper name was Griffin Memorial Hospital. All the individuals, druggies and genuine crazies alike, lived on eastside of town to easily acquire its services. Or, if there was severe weather like tornados, homeless could fake crazy and have a dry place to sleep for the night.

As Jesse passed it, he pondered again an old memory, one he wished not remember. He continued into the night, turning his head to the floor to evade the memories he'd attained from that asylum.

The only walkers who traveled the road across that mile stretch were druggies, tweaking on the poison in their veins; the homeless without a place to sleep, and the Young Detective with a tormented soul and the scars that fester him.

With the night drew a misty haze over the city which could only be formed by the devil himself. If the dark wasn't enough to hide his demon's misdeeds, the fog would better blanket their crimes. The Young Detective, the watcher of their sins, meant to unsheathe those sins. He'd meant to since the beginning. But, as the years carried on, and justice yet to prevail, he forgot his means to carry on. Why should he be the one to shovel around in the shit and grime of Norman, Oklahoma; nearly get himself killed, and in the process uncover the presence of a serial killer? He often asked himself: Why me? Without a moment's ponder, the answer rung true in his head: If not me, who else?

The trail he walked through the devil's haze was his burden, alone. As one foot stepped in shit, the other in grime, the Young Detective walked on with a dream of spring in his mind's eye.

His weary feet carried him along to the Headquarters where he found himself in his second office—atop the roof. Jesse looked over the city with the voice in his head quiet, for once void of lingering thoughts. The stillness in his head carried on just before dawn.

Just before the sky turned from a deep black into a blue hue, the sound of the door behind him creaking interrupted his silence. Jesse drew his attention to his visitor: Head Detective Harrison Wolfe.

"The kid who never learned how to die, I see." said he.

"I see your wife learned. I should ask her for some pointers, maybe I'll get off this rock sooner." Jesse turned back to the horizon.

Wolfe walked towards Jesse, every step echoing with aggressive vigor, "What the fuck did you just say to me, boy?" His suit was still stained with her blood, as well as splotches on his skin.

As Jesse felt his presence looming over him, he turned around with haste, the energy of rage with loomed over the detectives showing unadulterated through the stare in his eyes, "You sent me there to have me killed," Jesse exclaimed.

"He was going to kill my wife!" Wolfe's deep voice carried across the city.

Jesse turned his back to Wolfe once again, "The night your friend hung the Beaumont Girls," said he, "He visited my apartment—I'm assuming he's been watching me for quite some time, now. Trashed the place to hell. He left me a note, similar to the ones he leaves you. All it said was 'Dig'."

"You should've told me!"

"So you could lie to me again? You expect me to trust you even though you don't even trust me by letting me just look at the damn case file?"

"He stole the case--"

"I know he did—read about it in your diary, Wolfe," said Jesse, turning back to him. "I liked reading your diary. I thought I'd been losing my mind since that night on Beaumont. And reading your diary...it all suddenly made sense. Like pieces to a fucking puzzle falling in place."

Wolfe clutched his fists, raising them to his temple. "What I'm saying is, Wolfe, he had every intention to eventually kill your wife. He was just toying with you. If you read his letters, this man clearly has been plotting this for years. Hiding in the shadows until it was time for him to step into the light and by that time the darkness had consumed what was left of him. And you thought hiding his crimes was just going to make it all go away?"

Wolfe lowered his fists, with his head pointed down, he snarled at the Young Detective, "I would've killed you a thousand times over if it meant saving her. Your just some punk kid who waltz his way into my station only wanting to ever solve one cold case. You don't care about the greater good, you just want to know who burned all your friends alive. And then what? Ya gonna be the one to cuff him? You wouldn't even know where to look! But, if you hadn't've snubbed your nose where it didn't belong, I would've found a way out of this mess! So next time I ask you to grab the morning coffee like the bitch you are you should be thanking me I don't give you but an ounce of the shit I deal with daily!"

"It still would've been someone else doing your dirty work, Wolfe. Imagine being the man to let thirty-seven murders go unsolved and try to high road me about *the weight of the world*. You're nothing more than a bitch in that psycho's game!"

"Damn you," the veins in Wolfe's face throbbed, "ask yourself: In the world we live in...the hell does it matter anymore, Jesse? It's a war out there. Everyone's out there fighting for what little scraps are left and clinging on to the idea of the things that once were. Humanity is *animals*. What makes me any different? I chose my wife in this survival of the fittest. You're telling me you would've chosen some strangers from your past over family? I walk the same streets you do every fucking day. Would you give a bowl of beans to some homeless or your mother? As if your gratitude would matter, anyway."

"You have nothing left," Jesse noted.

"You're right," the look in Wolfe's eye became senile, "but now you and I are going to track that faceless son of a bitch to the ninth circle of Muslim Hell where I will slowly rip that bastard apart until even my soul is stained with his blood."

"You're right," said Jesse, "we are going to find him. But when the fog clears, and our man's mask sits on my desk, I will remind myself that you tried to send me to my death. My bullets beg to scatter your wagon-burning head, Harrison Wolfe. When it's all said and done, I'm going to kill you."

Wolfe walked back towards the door. He swung it wide open as the sky turned a blue hue. With one last glance, he said, "You better shoot straight," before slamming the door behind him.

12

Mended Scars

In the following days, as a phantom dawning a silver mask moved freely about, measures were taken. Rhodes, Wolfe, and even O'Massey were moved into safe houses on different sides of town. Wolfe was set up on a house on Lake Street on Eastside. O'Massey: A duplex down towards Noble. The Young Detective Jesse Rhodes had a house set up to himself on the outskirts on the north side of town, way out in the fields towards Moore.

Swiftly the public was made aware of the killer. First it became public knowledge of an attack on two detectives out on Campus Corner, then it was made known that one of those detectives was none other than the late Jesse Rhodes; back from the dead. In a message to the press, Jesse—mostly fabricating his story—told a tale of his findings about an apparent serial murderer on the loose. Beforehand, it was decided to keep it secret that the killer was only after the grown-up youth that happened to find themselves, tragically, in the Norman Church Fire some years ago. Public knowledge of it would only lead to protests and outrage since the killer was never found and is out to finish the job.

Doors were locked, people were frightened, the world was in shambles. Every fabric of the old world was being washed away before their eyes, and just to add to the terror of losing their homes to the Native Sieges, a killer may get to them first.

Jesse's thought on these things with much intensity. From the second story of that white house, sitting across a plain of field, he stood, deep in thought. The emotions of it all beat around inside him like a lightning bug trapped in a glass bottle. But on the outside, he showed not a hint of emotion. Just a plain slab of glass with no reflection; a mirror that doesn't look back.

The sun was setting. Pink and orange hues overlapped the blue and white in the sky. The warmth bounced off the window and glistened Jesse's face. It was the only thing he could feel, internally or externally.

To interrupt his silence, a familiar car shot up the gravel road leading to the house. With displeasure, Jesse chased down the stairs to meet it.

Before she could come up and knock, Jesse opened the screen door and met Allaura out on the porch. She had a breathtaking smile on her face, one Jesse knew too well, as he wore a sour grimace upon his. He had little time to react before her arms were wrapped around his neck and her chest pressed against his. "You did it!" she exclaimed in his ear.

Jesse was quick to push her off. "You need to leave!" he stated. He headed back inside the house, but Allaura was quick to follow.

"I'm not going anywhere, Jesse," she proclaimed. "You did it. You proved Dad didn't kill himself. It is just a matter of time before you bring down that rat bastard Wolfe! I cannot thank you enough!"

Jesse turned back to her; his snarl even more defined above his chin. "I didn't do it for you, you self-centered cunt," he said, "there's much more going on here than just your father's death, Allaura!"

Allaura pursed her lips, "He'll pay, won't he?"

"Don't worry about it. I'll handle Wolfe when the time comes." Jesse replied. "Now skip town, you're not safe here."

"Why?" Her eyes fell to the floor, "I... I just wanted to see you."

"There's a killer on the loose," said stared at the floor, "He's targeting us."

"Us?"

"The kids who survived the church fire."

"Huh? Wha-why?"

"We think it's the guy who set the fire in the first place...coming to finish the job."

"Why...what? Why would someone do that?" Allaura started to well up with emotion. The helplessness of a little girl looming in her eyes. "I can't leave you here, alone."

"...Goodbye, Allaura. Stay safe." Jesse turned to go back upstairs.

As his foot hit the first step, Allaura shouted, "Why after all this time are you still so cold to me?" Her voice cracked from the pain in her soul.

Jesse turned around and met her in the eye, "Excuse me?"

"You heard me, Jesse. You are so damn rude and I've done nothing but try to make keeping in contact with you work. I deserve to know what your problem is!"

The Young Detective stepped closer to her, his eyes terribly hiding the rage welling up in them. "After all you put me through, you have the nerve to ask me that?"

"After all *I* put *you* through? Jesse, look at all that we *went* through! I'm not the one who set that fire and damnit I wish I knew who did! I would've burned them alive myself like they did all our friends. Like they nearly did—"

"Please, don't say it." Jesse pleaded.

"Why can't you just accept it happened to us too? You parade around every day like the world happens to everyone but you—it's crippling you!"

"You think I asked for any of this?" said Jesse. "This isn't the life I planned to live, yet here I am, just trying to make the wrong things right. I wear that night on my back and I just want a normal day like everyone else. But everyday I'm reminded."

Allaura cascaded her gentle fingers down Jesse's cheek down to his chin. "When I was out partying...I was out there trying to make the wrong things right, too. An overdose later, things were still the same—worse, even. It took accepting the past, so it no longer affected my future did I start to sober up. And look at me now: I'm not married, I don't have as many kids as I'd like, yet, but I'm happy. I found a way to be happy, Jesse, and you of all people deserve that, too."

With a cold hand, Jesse lightly pulled her hand away from his face, staring blankly at her feet, "I never wanted any of this, Allaura. Back then, I'd imagined we'd be married by now. Living somewhere with a beach nearby. Not at war with each other with hearts full of resentment towards one another. It's all so wrong—everything's wrong!"

She shook her head, tears filling her eyes, "I don't resent you, Jesse. I feel bad for you. You have the weight of the world on your shoulders because you put it there. You didn't need to do all this. You didn't have to dedicate—"

"If I didn't, who would?" Jesse met her tearing eyes, "After a few weeks, a few candlelight services, a few T.V. spots, no one cared what happened to us. They just brushed it under the rug and didn't even bother to put the man who did it to justice. And I go to work, day-in and day-out, with those same men who didn't give a damn about us, and I have to find it within myself to *not* brutalize all of them for letting us all suffer without clarity!" Jesse turned pale red. His fists clinched and spittle flew from his lips as he yelled into her face. She stood there, calm, not swayed either way by his anger.

"I can't imagine how tough that must be," she said. "You, Jesse, are better than those men. You care. Probably too much. But you must let yourself realize what happened...happened."

Allaura took a step back from Jesse, eyes still locked. With one swift motion, she threw off her shirt and bra revealing herself to him. Jesse was taken back, his anger turned abruptly into blushing.

Across her voluptuous chest and torso, her skin remained untouched. From her forearms, her arms, all the way to her back, the skin was undoubtedly burned and scarred for life from it. Jesse knew the scars all too well.

He hadn't been so vulnerable. Just looking down at her in her perfections and her imperfections, the love he still had for her came to the forefront of his mind. As if suddenly all the bad times didn't matter anymore.

Rivers pours down his chin being wiped away by the cloth as he ripped away his shirt. Like her, his forearms were riddled with burn scars, as well as his back, from that retched fire that took the lives of so many.

Upon both their backs were two streaks where the skin was unharmed by the fire's hellish touch. With his heart heavy, Jesse wrapped around Allaura hugging her tightly. Where her scars ended on her back, his fell in unison along his forearms. Same way with the burns across his back as well. Flowing together in perfect alignment.

Jesse was overwhelmed. It had been too long since he'd allowed himself to yield to his emotional state. Rooted deep behind his angsty rage, his unhinged behavior, Jesse Rhodes was no more than a hurting boy trying to scrap back together the pieces of his wounded life. Same as Allaura, she was just better at accepting the reality.

At the height of their relationship, they'd spend most of their time together locked together in sensual hugs. No words spoken between them, not a single sway, just interlocked in each other's atmosphere. Soaking in the young love they'd shared for each other.

Before they knew it, it was already nightfall. The moon brought with it a cool breeze that infiltrated the screen door. With their burns showing something both of them tried carefully to hide, Jesse picked her up and carried her into the master room. With a bit of aggression, he threw her on the bed and then laid atop her. For the first time in years and leaned down and kissed her like he would've a lifetime ago.

He wanted to ravage her, and she him. But they knew there would be another time for it. They were drunk off the simple embrace alone. Like they were kids again, that's all they needed.

As the night deepened, the two drifted off into sleep still interlocked like strong magnets.

Jesse was awoken that morning by the sun shining into his eyes. Thinking he'd still be wrapped up in an old flame's embrace. He was left staring at the empty arms which only bared his immense pain. The backs of his forearms, the burns, he'd come to terms with, somewhat. From his wrists to the inside of his elbow he'd inflicted slashes with razor blades across years of torment. Waking up to the sight of those in the morning reminded him that the moment of relief he'd gotten was just that...a moment.

The Young Detective rolled from his bed, a looming sadness clouding his thoughts, and staggered to look from the window. Allaura was truly gone, her car no longer in the driveway.

He rolled out of bed and observed himself in the mirror. Rhodes never slept naked. He always had something to cover his body. Specifically, his arm. Though most of the scars he bore were inflicted upon him, the ones he couldn't stand being reminded of were the razor scars he gave to himself. Allaura would be in the room with him while he'd dig box cutter into his skin. All in an effort to numb the pain. But no cut was ever deep enough. In adulthood, the only true relief there is in the world is learning to feel nothing. Learn to be numb to it all.

The tears that flowed so easily the night before came of no avail that morning. Again, the wounds were left to fester with the bug in the glass bottle. With a sigh, Jesse slapped on his suit and headed out the door hopefully to catch the ripper in the silver mask.

13

Night of the Tornado

As the rains and the hail of Storm Season punished them, they grew no closer to finding the Ripper in the Silver Mask. Five months had passed, rolling into May, and they were no closer to him than Jesse and Wolfe were the night of Mrs. Wolfe's murder. Wolfe's guilt of that night lingered. So did Jesse's anger.

The public had thoroughly been warned of the killer's presence. Multiple interviews in the press given by both the Young and Old Detective. Norman watched in shock and shrill at Jesse's resurrection. Escaping the tyranny which occurred in Pauls Valley to come back home and tackle most likely the biggest case any of the detectives had touched since that retched church fire years ago.

The public across the metro boarded up their doors, if they had doors to board up. It wasn't made known the killer had a specific target—as per Wolfe's demand. Jesse thought it best otherwise, so possibly his targets could leave if they in fact still lived in the area. Wolfe argued the public knowledge would alert a city-wide outburst, be it, the case was unsolved and they're dealing with the man who lit the fire in the first place: reclaiming stolen trophies. Ultimately, it was Wolfe's call, he was still in charge.

Jesse was more than willing to let Wolfe have the petty victories. In the end, it didn't matter what the press knew, the public knew, or even what the killer knew; it was the Young Detective who was going to stand on top when the storm cleared. His trust wasn't in Wolfe or Shane. The only one he found an ounce of respect for was Buck.

One Sunday afternoon the Young Detective ventured down to Lexington where he found the fat bastard preaching his heart out to a group of less than twenty out at his church on Picketville Road. Buck already seen all the press coverage before Jesse had made contact with him; he wasn't shocked to see the young boy alive. Jesse, so calmly, asked him to join them on the task force, and with little hesitation, agreed.

Since the night of Mrs. Wolfe's death, Shane had been reluctant to speak to Jesse, much less look up to him as a superior on the case. When he was called in by the oinkers at the scene and they dropped Jesse's name, he called them all fools and made them leave. As he came in the next morning to see the Young Detective dismantling his desk and throwing his family photos in the toilet did he realize Jesse was alive and well.

Yet, all their collective minds combined, five months down the line, not a single suspect in the case—as was the church fire.

Jesse sat in the room with Wolfe, Buck and Shane, evidence and statements all laid out across the desks and the scattering the walls. He was transfixed in thought as the other detectives stifled through crime scene photos. He watched, collectively, their every move.

"Ya know, Kid," said Wolfe, not looking up from his papers, "we'd come up with something a lot faster if you'd help out."

"We're not gonna find out any more about him until he kills again. It's his move--he has all his pawns."

"So sure?" asked Wolfe.

"He hasn't been laying low since December because the heat is on him," replied Jesse, "He's preparing. This is methodical. He's been thinking about this for a while. Years maybe—in the shadows."

"Every man is sloppy. In here, he's made a mistake. Take his cough drop wrappers for instance—leaves 'em at every crime scene."

"It's a calling card, much like the notes he left you. It's all according to plan. Have you begged the question why he'd leave the wrappers at the scenes?"

"To tell us he has a cough?" Shane bugged in.

"...To tell you he's sick. Mentally. Physically, perhaps." Jesse stared at the papers on the wall. In the middle of the scattered evidence a sketch of the silver mask, as depicted by Wolfe and Jesse's accounts, was plastered. The Young Detective spent countless hours looking at it throughout the months.

"He did have a cough—just would sneak up on him, it seemed." Wolfe noted.

"My lungs betray me, sometimes," Buck added, "I used to work around fumes a bunch in my time in the Navy when I was Jesse, here's, age. All that junk gets stuck there and it stays there!"

"Perhaps he has prior military experience," Shane noted, "in the reports, I take it, he has some knowledge of defensive and offensive tactics."

"Yeah...something like that..." said Jesse, "Go down to highway nine, where the Satanists hang out. See if they have any ex-military among them—bring them in for interrogation."

"Would he be in his thirties," asked Shane, "since it is the same guy from the church fire. He'd be getting up there in age."

"As long as he's ex-military," Jesse replied.

"Buck, go with him," Wolfe added.

"I'll put the fear of my God into them," Buck shot from his chair; the chair screaming, "they'll know who the real God is by the end of it if it's the last thing I do!"

"Hopefully it isn't the last thing you do," said Jesse.

"Be back soon," said Wolfe, "It's gonna get pretty bad tonight I'd hate for you to get rained on by un-like-minded individuals."

Buck and Shane stormed out of the room. Their footsteps and the sound of the door echoed through the walls.

"Ya know, if you want to send my guys on a wild goose chase while you sit there with a fist up your ass how about you do it on someone else's dollar, eh?"

Jesse broke his concentration from the sketch on the wall and looked the old Wolfe in the eyes, "I know this man isn't a Satanist," he said, "but if he's trying to blend in with his anti-social behavior, that be the group to blend into. And you're right, there's no way this guy's military."

"Then what is he, Mister Detective, sir?"

"He's vengeful. His anger and hatred drives him." said Jesse. "And it's gotten him this far."

"How would you know that, Kid?"

"It's gotten me this far, hasn't it?" Jesse went back to contemplating the sketch.

As Wolfe was nose-deep in a case file, thunder rolled across the sky—the sound went off like an explosion. It was so ghastly it broke both men's concentrations in unison. They looked towards the nearest window. The sky turned greyer and greyer, almost black. The first sprinkles of a monstrous storm made way to the Norman streets.

Jesse got up and stepped over to the glass panels and tilted his head up. The sky was eclipsed by gray and white plumes puffed into balls. On the horizon the gray and white formed a vast pillar which spanned across the sky. "Yeah, Shane and Buck are going to be warmed up to Satanists for the night," said Jesse.

Wolfe approached the window and gave the sky his own observation. "Get back to your safe house for the night, Kid. Last place I want to get stuck for the night is here." Wolfe fumbled into his office, grabbed his suitcase, and stormed out of the building.

Jesse gathered his things and placed them on his desk. Before he retreated from the storm, he made his way to the roof. The breeze was an icy chill nipping at his neck when blowing east, then a warm haze when the wind reverted west.

Even in with the pending storm, Jesse's mind worried more on the case. Looking across the landscape, it irked him knowing somewhere behind a tree or in a house, or crept behind some bush, this killer was out there. The fire in his belly roared the more he thought of him; regardless he thought about him constantly. The Young Detective's entire young life was devoted to finding the arsonist who burned alive some of his closest friends...now a man, be it the same man, wants to finish the rest of them off. Each move Jesse made, or allowed Wolfe to make, was vital to the survival of the players in the game. The most dangerous game of chess, where the pawns are all that matter.

Each day ticked and the killer's silence spoke so paramount to him it was more like a lioness' roar. He knew he was planning something; he just didn't know what. And, to add to his frustration, he wouldn't know until he'd already done it.

Lightning struck the ground in the distance. As the thunder shrieked across town, Jesse departed off the roof and headed for his safe house. With haste, Jesse sped up 12th Street which converted into Sooner Road the closer he got to the outskirts of Moore. His safe house was off a country road between Norman and Moore perched up on a small hill with roughly twelve acres of land.

With his driving, he was there in five minutes on the fifteen-minute journey. He beat the heavy rain by a minute or more. By the time he was on his porch the heavy rain had started pouring. Within minutes the sky was a hazy black and mid-afternoon was dead of night. An orange hue loomed the atmosphere as more thunder rocked the trees and sky.

While viewing the storm from the porch, from Moore to Norman, the tornado sirens yelled their warnings.

Growing up there, he knew sometimes—most of the time—the sirens cried wolf. His instinct told him otherwise. Jesse headed into his safe house for blankets and pillows then proceeded into the cellar which sat off-center in the back yard. He wasn't going to risk being sucked away by a tornado when a serial killer is running around.

Jesse slammed the cellar doors. His only friends were the four concrete slabs which made up the walls and the one slab which stuck out that made up the stool.

With the sirens still screaming and the rain thumping down on the cellar surface, sleep wasn't an option. To add to the dismay, hail escaped the clouds raining down pounding and pounding on the cellar.

Like circles in his head, his mind drifted towards the case. The storm roared over him, causing a ringing in his ear. He blurred out the noises; focused his mind on the man in the silver mask. He thought on it so much, his mind zoned out the lightning, the thunder, the hail, he was completely in his own world. He could see every bit of evidence like it laid out in front of him there in that tiny cellar.

The Young Detective felt in jerk in his stomach. The thought that the man who set that church on fire all those years ago was back kill the rest of them. It was like his whole upbringing was preparing him for this moment. Jesse Rhodes couldn't save his friends back then...he'd be damned if he didn't save them now.

Hours fell by the wayside. The storm was far from over. By ten or so, Jesse was getting antsy inside the storm cellar. In the dead of night, Jesse swung open the door and fell back inside the house thinking he was in the clear. Rain was still plummeting to Earth rapidly; the hail scattered the ground like golf balls on the green. Jesse made his way to the porch to get a better look at the storm.

As he turned the knob, the aggressive wind robbing the door from his grasp and swung open by itself. With more strength Jesse closed it behind him as to not lose it again.

Lightning flashed the sky with a blue hue before the rumble of thunder called to the heavens. In those moments of flashing blue light, the monster which plagued the prairie for centuries showed its might.

It was a skinny one, nonetheless, but still ferocious. A cloud with a thin funnel and a wide base descended down on top of Norman, it looked like to Jesse. Lightning flashed again and he caught a better glimpse of it. It was heading eastbound; nowhere in his vicinity.

The sirens were still ablaze from Slaughterville to Oklahoma City: a warning of homes and businesses' pending doom. Where others would run and hide away in their cellars, Jesse stayed perched on the white, wooden porch contemplating the tornado. As if it were not a natural disaster happening before his eyes, but rather a phenomenon only to be witnessed by the few in their lifetime.

Within the hour, the tornado swallowed back up into the sky and only rain and lightning left to torment the city. Jesse was lightly drenched from the rainwater splashing up onto the porch hitting him across his body. He seemed oblivious to it—lost in his own mind his body was numb to the elements. He went back inside, loosely drying his skin, then fell into the bed in the master bedroom at the back of the house.

In his dreams he was tormented by better days. Like the ones he used to share with Allaura, his father and mother. They picked at him because he knew those days were long past, never to be rekindled like the flame that raged in his heart...

...An orange-sky-morning glistened over The Metro. Jesse was awoken by his alarm and his phone ringing simultaneously. He shut off the alarm, then answered the phone to an irate Wolfe on the other end.

"Yeah?" he said, groggily.

"Parrington Oval. Get your ass down here—hurry!" Wolfe hung up the phone.

Whatever tiredness betrayed him in that moment, he made it submit. The Young Detective rushed out of bed, staggered into his suit and peacoat and rushed for the door. With grim, gray clouds overhead Jesse raced to the university in the heart of town.

His face sunk down to his gut as he pulled to the corner of Boyd and Parrington. The two streets were sandwiched between Campus Coner and Campus itself; it was already swarming with cops by the time Jesse pulled up. Beyond the round-about, he could see Wolfe with an elongated face marching around one of the statues.

The state itself was one of the more admired deans of the University. He was commemorated forever sitting down looking forward—to the future—some would argue. As Jesse drew closer, with haste, he could see what the commotion was about.

Perched in the statue's lap laid the body of a naked female. Her hands still bound by her attacker and eyes blindfolded with a black cloth. Her upper and lower halves were separated, guts falling out onto the lap, yet the killer laid her in the fetal position like a babe in her mother's arms.

Jesse caught eyes of it and froze in his footsteps. To gaze it was just enough to send a man over the edge. Uneasy stomachs were gathered all around. Wolfe, who stood closest to it, had his eyes fixated on it. Like he wouldn't let himself look away. Over the garden square, in the center of the oval, another statue laid; another valiant member of the university. Another swarm of cops were surrounding it, observing its inhabitants. Jesse raced over to it. *Surely,* he thought, *it can't be.*

The statue of the man was standing upright. With wrists bound, the male corpse with noticeable burn scars across what was his torso and neck hung off the statue's neck like a necklace. Like the other victim, his eyes were covered with a black cloth.

Jesse's eyes sank into their sockets; his gut plunged to earth. Shane O'Massey was looking up at the body. With the decades he'd put into the job, same with Wolfe, they'd thought they'd seen everything. The devil laughed and said, "Not yet."

Shane broke his gaze from the statue, turned to the Young Detective and said, "There's another one on the Sphinx at the museum...Buck is there—another male victim."

"Three in a night?" Jesse blurted out.

"Do you recognize him?" asked Shane.

Jesse looked up at the corpse, the hardest stare of him life. "No, I suppose not anymore." he said, truthfully.

"No I.D.s on any of the bodies," he said, "there's burn marks on all of them indicating..."

"There's no way they could've called for help--"

"Because the tornado—thing traveled down highway nine then sucked back into the air. We questioned the--"

"Not now, Shane." Jesse interrupted.

"Rhodes!" Wolfe chased towards the Young Detective, a phone in his hand as if he'd just gotten off the phone.

Jesse turned around to meet him, "We just got a call—corner of Classen and 12th...there's another one."

That was no more than a quarter mile from Parrington Oval. Close to where the Beaumont Girls were. Jesse ran back to his car and wasted little time getting there. To meet him there was already a plethora of cops and forensics.

In the general area was a supermarket, a convenience store, motels, and some apartment complexes which were about a minute away from Jesse's old one. The swarm was gathered on the corner of one of the complexes which was just an open field with a plaque that read: "Welcome to Norman est. 1889". The Young Detective shoved forensics and cops from his path and looked down at the sign. Laid at the foot of it, arms spread, and legs together pointed out, a female body laid. Her eyes were covered with black cloth. "Oh, shit." Jesse muttered.

"No I.D," said a female officer, "but we found this."

With a gloved hand she handed him a brown envelope—sealed. It had residue of red and black splotched on it. He took it from her and looked at it. In red the letter "S" was written. Specifically for Detective Jesse Rhodes.

Jesse opened it with shakiness in his hands. The letter read:

Dear Mr. Detective Jesse Rhodes of Normantown,

The weather was just too lovely—the temptation overwhelmed me. I bet you're delighted to hear from me, again. Afterall, it has been your life's work. Don't worry, you won't have to wait another five months for me to act out God's plan. He was antsier than I was, honestly.

I'm ashamed to note you're department didn't warn these lovelies of my intentions. They welcomed me in with open arms, offered me warmth and shelter to wait about the storm—then God struck. I assumed they would've been waiting for me to knock on their doors and have the shotgun ready. Failures, failures. This town is full of them.

I was delighted to see that God put your name on my list. It all makes sense, now. You'll be the last, of course. I see you didn't make the same mistake Wolfe did and you got your family out of town. It's a pity. I would've loved picking little lily flowers out of my garden if you know what I'm saying.

Jesse crumbled the paper in his hand. "YOU FUCKING BASTARD!" He screamed to the gray sky. His face was hot, fumed escaped from his temple as he stood over the body.

A male cope ran up to the fuming detective. "Detective!" he shouted. "I was a witness here who says she caught the guy on camera."

"Take me to her!" he yelled.

The cop led him across the street to the second story of one of the complexes. He took him to the door of an elderly woman, her body riddled with shakes. She had in her hands an older generation smart phone, with her bony fingers she scrolled to the video.

Before his own eyes, the woman had recorded in the dead of night, the storm guzzling down over him, the man with the silver mask placing the woman's body at the foot of the plaque. "Why didn't you call us last night, ma'am?" Jesse tried not to sound bashful with rage.

"I-I did, sir, honest," said she, "I couldn't get through—the lines were down!"

"Officer, bag this phone for evidence!" Jesse commanded as he headed back down across the streets, stomping with every step.

Jesse's phone alarmed in his pocket. Grasping for it, he nearly crumbled it in his hand. "What!" he yelled into the phone. Wolfe was on the other end, "Fifth one—on the Seed Sower."

"Five... we let him get away with five?" Jesse said after a silence.

Wolfe hung the phone up on the Young Detective. He could barely fathom a thought through his anger. In the five months without a trace, they let five more slip through their fingers. And there was plenty more to come...

14

The Witness & The Missing Person

The five bodies were autopsied and cause of death was determined all before the sun rose the next morning. Five out of five: strangulation was the cause—no prints were found. Minutes after the body was discovered that morning, the entire metro from Noble to Edmond was put on lockdown. From the video the elderly took the detectives deduced the time of night was right as the tornado was ripping through Highway Nine at around one in the morning. Since that highway is the only access point to the main interstate through the southside of town.

After a forty-eight-hour lockdown, he wasn't found. Shortly after his displays were put up, he must've hit Interstate Thirty-five. From there he could've gone all the way to Denver or St. Louis of he wanted to—be long detached from his crimes.

In the days that followed, Shane O'Massey and Spergeon "Buck" Jordan spent countless hours, day and night, looking for the group of Satanist that they'd encountered before the storm. One of them, Shane as described as a bald girl with pale white skin, said she'd seen the car hanging around their camp. She was willing to go with them for an interview as long as she got a bite to eat, but as soon as the weather turned, they all split.

While Buck and O'Massey were out searching, Wolfe and Rhodes were locked away at headquarters with photos and statements of the crime scatters across desks, floors and walls. The room was dark so the projector could play the old woman's video back-to-back on a loop. Jesse Rhodes viewed the footage mercilessly, against his own will—it tormented him.

What got to Jesse the most was seeing his younger sister's name appear on the Silver-Faced Ripper's egregious note to him. It brought about even more hatred for this masked coward. Little did the Rippler know, the fire that burned within Jesse was ready to come out and burn him, it was only a matter of time.

Shane and Buck, sweaty and wheezy threw light into the room as they kicked the door open. "We...we found her!" Exclaimed Buck in his deep, preacher-bass voice.

Without a glimpse of hesitation, "I'll talk to her!" Jesse rushed out the door.

"Room seven!" Buck yelled down the hall; Rhodes was already nearly passed the room.

To the girl's surprise, Jesse rushed through the door, it hitting the back wall he opened it so fiercely. She jumped back, the look on Jesse's face as he walked in didn't ease her fright. Jesse shut the door behind him, as he was turned away he noticed her instant discomfort—he rearranged his demeanor.

"Can I have your name, please?" He began, "My name is Detective Jesse Rhodes."

"Staar Morse—I go by Freya." she said.

He couldn't help but notice the girl's similarity to Allaura. In the face from the nose-up, they were almost an identical match. Her pale skin and her skinny-as-a-rail body were different, but he felt somewhat familiar with her in that sense.

"Freya? Isn't that Pagan?" Jesse noted.

"Yeah, so?" she replied with defense in her tone.

"No means to offend," Jesse threw his hands up, "I was just curious to how the nickname came about."

"Oh, sorry," said the girl, "I just thought it sounded cool. Better than the one my mom gave me."

"What's wrong with Staar?"

"I just hate the name...and my mother."

Jesse tried his best to look sympathetic to her, but it only came off as disinterested. "I see," he said, "Now, Freya, I understand you came across our beige sedan we've been keeping our eyes out for, is that right?"

"Yeah...I've seen it—been seeing it—for quite a while, actually."

"Across your campsite down by the highway, correct?" Jesse pried a bit more.

"We have others across town, but yeah, that one." she replied.

Jesse noted the purple droops under her eyes. The whites of them were shot red. As he was pulling out his journal, Wolfe walked into the observation room to eye in on his questioning.

"Where are these other camps?" asked Jesse bringing his pen to his paper.

"...I don't remember." said Staar.

"Ms. Freya..." Jesse looked up at her; she was itching at her neck with one hand and with the other she was reaching over to itch her forearm. When Jesse tried to look her in the eye, she knelt her head down looking at the floor. "...Has he showed up at these other campsites?"

"Y-yeah..."

"And, for a fact, this person was driving a beige four-door?" Jesse added.

"For sure, I think I sat in it, once." she was hesitant to say.

"What did this person look like? The one driving the beige car?"

"I don't know...he always wore a mask. L-like it's still twenty-twenty, or something." Staar drew a half smile as if trying to be light-hearted.

"How old were you, then? If I may ask." Jesse changed the subject entirely.

"Fourteen, how old were you?"

"I was nineteen. I'm twenty-five, now. So, I take it, Freya, you're twenty?"

"Nineteen--I don't turn twenty until October." she corrected.

"How long have you been doing drugs?"

Staar halted her scratching. For the first time in the interview she locked eyes with Detective Rhodes. "I-I-"

"It's okay, Staar. I don't mean to offend. I also have no interest in arresting you. See, personally, I don't care what you're doing to yourself, or how hard your loved ones cry for you every night you go burn pentagrams and shoot up heroin—I'm assuming it's heroin. I personally, am hunting down a psychopath who has called me out by name. I'm sure you'll get busted at some point in your life with a teenth shoved up your ass, but at this point that's not my problem. Tell me what you know."

Staar slid down in her chair. Her fingers clamed up as she looked down at the table trying to gather up a sentence with her altered brain. "...He'd come around every few weeks. He said he's from out of town. He wasn't a Satanist—he'd always debate some of the other guys about their beliefs. We bought from the same guy, but he'd never shoot up with any of us—just buy his shit, camp out with us, be gone after a few days."

"And the entire time he was wearing a mask? You never saw any bit of his face?"

"He wore it up to his nose, but I could see the bridge-up."

"How old would you say he looked?" Jesse continued with the notes in his journal.

"...I couldn't tell you...the right side of his face, I guess he looked kinda young. But the left side looked mauled. Like he'd been attacked by something."

"How disfigured was he? Was his left eye still there but the skin around it was drooped down—looked like the skin melted down over it."

"Melted..." Jesse wrote the word in bold on the page.

"He gave us a name too."

Jesse, with a chill up his spine, looked up at the girl. "Tell me."

"...He said his name was Jesse."

Wolfe and Jesse both halted in their shoes when she gave the name. "Staar... are you sure that's the name he said?"

"Yeah...the guys were prying him after a bit. At first he gave them a street name, but they kept badgering him."

"What was the street name?"

"Alter...like 'alter ego'."

Jesse wrote the word down in his notes. His eyes jumped from note-to-note across the page like putting together pieces to the puzzle in his head. He placed the pen down in the fold of the book and closed it. "I'm going to have you speak to a sketch artist. Whenever he comes, he'll get you that meal. Thank you for your time, Freya."

As Jesse was stepping out, Wolfe was in sync, stepping out of the observation room as well. Just when Jesse had his hand on the knob, Buck with his wide gut busts through the door nearly sending the Young Detective back against the table.

"What?!" Jesse shouted.

"We just got a call in—girl's gone missing—said the mother found a note on her bed." Buck's voice was frantic.

"A suicide note?"

"No...one of *his* notes."

Jesse's eyes filled with heaps of fire. "Get a sketch artist in here for her—what's the address?" The Young Detective raced passed Buck, meeting Wolfe in the hallway.

"Fourteen Eighteen Boyd Street."

Wolfe and Rhodes raced to the cars. By the time they pulled up to the house two units were already inside the house and Shane just beat them to the house by a millisecond. Jesse nearly forgot to put his car out of gear he was in such a hurry.

Two cops on scene were standing at the door while another two were inside. "Update me," Jesse snarled at them.

"Gotta call from the mother about a wellness check; we show up ain't no girl but the door's wide open. We enter—note on the bed—we called you." the cop explained while he walked Jesse into the back bedroom.

"She got a name?"

"Crawford. Kaytlynn Crawford."

Just like the two girls and Beaumont, and the bodies on the statues, Jesse was familiar with the name.

"Notify the mother. Bring her in for questioning immediately." Said Jesse looking down at the bed. "Gloves."

The bed was neatly made; the note was placed at the foot under a blanket folded into a square.

Rhodes was the single word written on the envelope. As soon as the piglet came back with a pair of vinyl gloves, Jesse opened the letter and read it to himself:

> She didn't put up much of a fight. I was hoping for a few scratches at least. She won't stop crying, but that's okay. You should be proud, she thinks you're gonna save her. What I didn't tell her, only God can save her. But even he's too scared of his own creation to get in my way. Funny. The creator himself can't even sleep in the bed he made...
>
> Consider the scriptures, Detective Rhodes,

Numbers 34:9

Proverbs 4:3

Psalms 45:6

Judges 9:7

2 Samuel 2:20

Leviticus 7:36

Rhodes, having not practiced the religion in years, didn't know any scriptures by memory. Wolfe came up from behind and ripped the note from his hand. "You need to give that to Buck," said Rhodes.

Wolfe skimmed over the letter. Buck and Shane piled into the room each applying gloves. A look of worry filled their eyes. Wolfe locked the note between two of his fingers and extended his arm out to Buck, "That's all you," Wolfe said.

Buck looked over the note, Shane looking over his shoulder. "I'd have to write the scriptures down," he said, "but, Lord willing, I can deduce this."

"He's toying with us," said Rhodes, "this is a game to him."

"For all we know, that girl is still alive," Wolfe said. "We need to figure this out as soon as possible—get an amber alert out. I want this girl's face on every T.V. in a hundred-mile radius."

Rhodes filed out of the room. Shane followed him. "What did we find out from that girl?"

"Our guy has a burned face. Also, he buys heroin."

"No way this guy is doing all this while on a trip." Shane said.

"He's not. This is too precise. It's for someone else." said Rhodes.

By nightfall, Kaytlynn Crawford's face was at the forefront of every news circuit in the metro and beyond. Calls flooded their department on possible sightings, and each was followed up on, but they didn't lead to her finding.

From the rooftop of headquarters, Jesse Rhodes watched the sun set. The weight of the city rested on his shoulders. He considered the note, and for once, he agreed with the killer on something: God couldn't sleep in the bed he made...it was up to men like Rhodes to make it for him. All in hopes of a better tomorrow.

15

Rhodes Wishes He Was Wrong

Staar's sketch was plastered all over town. It looked eerily familiar to Rhodes; almost like a forgotten memory. Maybe he'd seen him on the street prancing around the university or passing by at one of the old shopping areas. It must've been some years since.

Buck had found and written down every scripture on the note left at the Crawford house. Altogether, the scriptures made no sense, biblically or otherwise. He, with all his knowledge of Christ and his teachings, couldn't make heads or tails of what this psychopath was trying to get at.

Shane continued interviewing locals saying they'd seen suspicious characters looming about. But this was post-rescission Norman, almost everyone was a shady character. Picking out which one was the "shady character" they were looking for, that was like finding a needle in a stack of other needles.

"Tell me, Wolfe," said Jesse, eyeing the sketch, "how does a murderer know the addresses of every victim of the Church Fire, and we don't have a single record of any of them?"

"They couldn't have been in the case file, which I know he has them," said Wolfe, "the bastard stole it from Brent's safe. Damn fool. They were better kept here."

"So you'd think," said Rhodes. "How'd he know they were with him to begin with?"

"...What're you getting at?" asked Wolfe as Buck was crossing out words from the scripture.

"Someone told him—or is telling him." said Rhodes. "Where would the names and addresses of all the victims be?"

"Whenever the fire happened, most of the children, including you, I think, were taken to Griffin Memorial."

"No," corrected Rhodes, "Allaura and I were flown to OKC. Our skin melted onto one another. They had to detach us like conjoined-fucking-twins."

"I remember when the helicopter came," added Buck.

"No shit," said Wolfe giving Buck a grimaced stare.

"How many of the victims were taken to Griffin as opposed to Norman General?"

"At the time, if I remember right, Griffin had more space. Less influx of crazies at that time, I guess. When I got there, I was just helping put kids in ambulances."

"I hate thinkin' on that day," said Buck, "I wish I could unsee all that."

Rhodes look off his jacket and rolled up his sleeves. He stood over Buck whose head was buried deep into his Bible and notes. Rhodes slapped the table, getting his attention. He rose up his forearms giving Buck a long look. "I lived it. I think about it everyday. And everyday following I trusted you fuckers to figure out who burned me. Now, here I am, seven years later doing your fucking job. Now read your damn Bible and ask your God for clairvoyance."

"You are not gonna stand there and talk to me that way!" Buck shouted with a voice that carried all the way to the basement.

Wolfe stood up, Rhodes had already turned his back to Buck, staring back at the projector.

"Seven fucking years," Rhodes muttered. "How long afterwards did you guys decide the case was cold?"

"Buck..." said Wolfe, sticking out a hand.

"We didn't decide it—nothing!" Buck shouted. "The D.A. told us to focus on more recent crimes. Now I know you got a lot of pent-up anger for what happened to you, boy, but between me and God Almighty, I did everything in my power to find that damn devil!"

"Wolfe?" said Rhodes.

"We interrogated over two-hundred residents. Nothing came up. D.A. decided it was a waste of money and efforts, they wouldn't let us touch the case, anymore. That's why Brent took the case files to his house. He'd work on it every chance he could. Goodman and I would even go over there and help him, but he was no detective. He didn't know where to begin, he just...wanted to avenge his daughter. And, I guess, you."

"You never told our boy about Brent and the case files being there, did you?"

"No." said Wolfe. "He never asked."

"He never asked you." said Rhodes. "Because he already knew where they were."

"By who—" As the question left his lips, he knew what Jesse was getting at, "Listen here, kid, that's one of my best friends you're talking about. You're crossing a fucking line!"

"Think about it, Wolfe," said the Young Detective, "He started blackmailing you months before Brent was killed, right. How long was it before that did Jeff Goodman go missing?"

"Some months," said Wolfe, "you don't think?"

"I think you weren't his first detective to blackmail. I think before you, Goodman was his guy. He gave him the information, he possibly is the one who gave him the list of names of all the children who were there that night in the fire. And once he was done with him or retaliated... that's when he started blackmailing you."

"That son of a bitch!" Wolfe threw down his fedora. "That bastard!"

"We need to figure out where Jeff Godman went the day he went missing." said Rhodes.

"I remember that day," said Buck, "Last day I saw him, he left with a bunch of files tucked under his arm. Said he was heading north to meet a friend of his about an old case. Oh, my word, I should've known!"

"North? Where's North? Tulsa? Oklahoma City?" Jesse scratched his lip.

"No Man's Land," said Wolfe, "He said 'No Man's Land' in his last diary entry."

"The Panhandle?" said Jesse.

"That's all Cartel Territory, now." said Buck

"We can't just get into No Man's Land without getting rung up with Mexican bullets." said Wolfe.

"Damn it!" Jesse shouted in frustration.

"I'll have to pull some strings with the D.A., see if I can get us safe passage into the panhandle. I don't even know where'd we begin to look."

"Buck," said Rhodes, "You and Shane go to Griffin Memorial. Ask them about Goodman. Pull the exact same files he did, if he did pull any, for that matter."

"Shane's up in the interrogation room. I'll go pull him."

Buck stormed out of the room. Wolfe proceeded to follow him, possibly to make some calls about their new endeavor into the Panhandle. "Stay," said Rhodes.

Wolfe stopped for a moment, "Yeah?" he said.

"You were listening to my interview with the satanist girl, right?"

"Yeah, I was." said Wolfe.

"You hear the name she said our guy was passing around?"

"Yeah, 'Jesse.'"

"No, the other one," said Rhodes, "Alter."

"What're you getting at?"

"Alter was the name of our youth group. 'The Alter Youth'"

"So he's taunting you and the kids in the fire. He must really hate you guys for some reason. That's why he burned it down in the first—"

"It's not the same guy, Wolfe," corrected Jesse, " When Buck comes back with the list of names of the kids taken to Griffin Memorial, we'll find all the names of our current victims...as well as the killer, himself."

"What the fuck are you getting at, Kid?"

Jesse turned around and met him eye-to-eye. He could tell Wolfe could only half-comprehend what he was trying to say. "He said he was gonna burn down the same city that burned him to feel it's warmth. We're not dealing with a man who burned down the church, we're dealing with a man who got burned by the church!"

"So, you're telling me, you think, that the original killer is long gone? And in his absence and new monster arose from the ashes he left behind?"

"Our list of victims will align with all the kids who were taken to Griffin. And from then-on we can find a suspect."

"You're wrong..." Wolfe's face flushed red; his eyes welled up, "God, I hope you're wrong."

"Me, too."

Wolfe opened the door, "I'll go make some calls."

16

The Vast

The day dimmed to the end. Buck spent hours at the Griffin Memorial with O'Massey while Wolfe made phone calls. Jesse didn't do much else besides feeling tormented by his own gut-feeling. As the sun set, Jesse went back home.

He pulled into that gravel driveway, bags looming under his eyes. Exhaustion pressed him to sleep but anxiety fought him awake. He couldn't get a peaceful rest before pointing a gun in every closet and corner of the house. Once that was done, he locked himself away in the upstairs bedroom with the gun on the nightstand.

Since she went away, he'd wished her by his side. He wished he had her to hold so his mind wouldn't drift away, back into the fire or deep within his self-loathing. Back then, the razor cuts on his arms kept him from doing that. But eventually, like everything else, he grew numb to it.

It was nine or so, his mind was still dancing with pain and grief. Sleep, like many other nights was alluding him. Before his tears could put him to rest, lights shined through the window glaring into his eyes. A great whooshing sound, like a loud fan, rung his ears as he shot up and reached for the gun. He checked outside through the blinds. Right by his car, in the grass, a helicopter was landing down. Once it landed, two men in suits stormed out heading for the house.

Jesse rushed downstairs to meet them, gun in hand. Before one could knock, he swung open the door keeping the gun at his side.

"The governor would like a word with you!" One man shouted over the noise of the chopper.

The words took the Young Detective back. The men allowed Jesse to put on proper attire, then they rushed him into the helicopter and flew off.

The helicopter ride was no more than fifteen minutes, due north. From the window Jesse could tell they were making way for the skyline of Oklahoma City. The chopper landed on the helipad atop Devon Tower—the tallest building in all the state. They escorted him inside down to the forty-ninth floor.

The forty-ninth floor was a restaurant known as "The Vast". It was higher-end, Rhodes heard it had shut down after the economy went to shit. Women and men dressed in cheap suit and ties led Jesse and the men down the hall into the main dining area. Only one man was seated in the entire establishment.

"Have the scallops, they're super!" said the man to Jesse, who hadn't even sat down yet or anywhere near the table, rather.

Jesse approached the table, slowly. The older man, balding, chubby, and a bit pale was cutting into a steak like salivating over it before it even reached his mouth. "I eat here every night," he said as Jesse sat down, "one of the many, many perks."

"Wouldn't suppose there's enough food in here to feed the rest of Oklahoma City," said Jesse, "or the rest of *our* state for that matter."

"They couldn't afford it." said Governor Kevin Britt. "I can't believe who I'm looking at right now! *Detective* Jesse Rhodes—survived getting killed in Pauls Valley to hunt down a serial killer. Why haven't we met, yet?"

"I've been busy," replied Jesse. "I'm sure you're a busy man, yourself."

"Been doing great work for my beloved state, I assure you!" he said laughing as chunks of steak fell from his mouth. "Here, I ordered you scallops."

A waitress poured Jesse a glass of red wine as another brought him a full plate of scallops. Before the dish was even properly on the table, the Governor dug his fork into it and shoveled the bite into his mouth. "Always gotta take the taxes out!" he snickered.

Watching the man eat made Jesse's hunger go from non-existent to obsolete. Jesse pushed away the plate, "Would you happen to have beans? I've grown accustomed to the taste since it's the only affordable food in this country."

The Governor looked down at the full plate and then up at the detective. "Well, sure," he said, "but I don't see why you wouldn't want to indulge. You'll probably never see another scallop in your lifetime."

"Just like the people in Oklahoma who will never see their homes again in their lifetime, right?" Jesse scolded the man as he was face down in mashed potatoes.

"I know," said Kevin Britt, "isn't that a shame?"

"Why am I here?"

"Your department called me," said the governor, "you--gah—say you have a lead in the panhandle. I'm afraid through the laws of jurisdiction...we, the governor's office can't allow for all that—jurisdiction like I said; nothing I can do."

"Have you tried trying?" Jesse's face was stern and uncaring.

"It's not that simple, Mr. Rhodes—"

"Detective Rhodes," he corrected.

"Sorry, *Detective Rhodes*—it's not that simple. The Complexities of the situation are not as forthright as some would seem."

"If our man is in the panhandle, there's nothing stopping him from coming back down to the metro and killing again," Jesse further ignored the plate of hot food. The smell was like his mother's fresh bread in the morning; like a soothing memory."

"Pity. Try the wine. I sense you're upset."

"You're sitting here with your steaks and your fucking scallops while good men and women out there are shoveling shit for nickels? Those good people are relying on you to fix this mess."

"This isn't even what I brought you here to talk about, Detective." the governor said sternly. "You're here to discuss No Man's Land."

"Jurisdiction. I'm a fucking detective. I don't have jurisdiction. Why are you wasting my time?" Jesse leaned forward trying to meet Governor Britt's eyes.

Staring down at his steak, the leader of the state chuckled. Placing down his fork, he looked up at Jesse with an unnerving grin.

"I guess youth doesn't equal ignorance," said Britt. "Have some wine."

"I don't want your fucking wine or your dinner, Britt. Stuff yourself while the rest of us starve. I'm sure there's a special spot in hell for you," Jesse got up from the table.

"Shame. Maybe in the near future I could've helped you find out whoever burned down that crappy, old church."

Jesse flung back around in a hurry, "What the hell did you just say?"

"You know, your friend, Wolfe, he was close to cracking the case at one point. But, evidently, his department ran out of resources to keep the case going. Do you know why his department lost funding for such a state-wide tragedy?"

"Why is that, Governor Britt?"

With his head pointed down and eyes pointing up like a lion locked on to prey, he spoke, "Because none of them would drink the wine."

"Goodnight, Governor. I'll find my own way back home."

"Ha! Pity."

The Young Detective retreated into the elevator as quick as he could. "Nasty, old, bastard." Jesse felt like he needed a shower, instantly.

He made it to the base floor and marched out the building. Hoping, perhaps, he'd find a taxi back home. Jesse walked for a few blocks, there was no one on the road except sleeping homeless folk. The streets had been trashed and brick walls were falling off their structure. The city he once knew was long gone. The city he once knew was just one, big ghetto.

After an hour walk, Jesse came up on a police station. It's not like the cops inside didn't already know his face. To be courteous, he flashed them his badge and asked them for a ride back down to Moore. One cruiser agreed and let him hitch a ride.

17

Confirmation

"We had to go back 'n' look at over a year's worth of footage. But, we got it!" Buck rushed in the room that morning. He'd stayed the night at Griffin Memorial Hospital with O'Massey by his side. They stifled through the footage in shifts from five p.m., when Rhodes left, to that morning at nine 'o' clock. To say they were as tired as old dogs was an understatement.

Shane nearly dosed off, Buck actually did dose off, while Wolfe and Rhodes picked through the files.

"This is what Goodman gave to our killer." said Rhodes.

"Whatever he held over his head—he should've told me!" Wolfe hit the desk with his fist.

Upon opening the file they found exactly what Rhodes had deduced. A year ago, Detective Jeff Goodman—days before his disappearance—inquired the medical records of all the children in the Norman Church Fire that were brought to Griffin Memorial Hospital just off 12th Avenue. Thirty-seven teens and younger were transported from the church to that hospital.

Each page gave an account of their medical history, the wounds they suffered, where they suffered the wounds, their ages, and the severity of their injuries. The page also contained photographs of the injuries treated for.

"The addresses on these are dated," said Wolfe, "See, that's not the Beaumont address."

"He must've been stalking them for quite some time. That's their parents' addresses." said Rhodes.

"These victims from the university statues, Makayla Teal, Grace Smith, Theo Seldom, Ashley DeCoupe, Brett Loggin. They're all here, as well," cried Wolfe.

"He must be in here, too." Jesse grabbed the file off the desk and started pulling out pages. "We can rule out the victims...and the women. We know that much. That leaves...nineteen."

"We know his face was burned in the fire, how many suffered that?" Wolfe pulled the file down reading each male victim's injury report.

"I remember seeing a lot of burning bodies running around," said Jesse, "I couldn't tell you which ones. To be honest, none of these names sound familiar except maybe two."

"Which two?" asked Wolfe.

Jesse turned to their files, "Rustan, he was just fourteen. Wasn't a bad kid, little annoying at times. He was one of the firsts to make it out, though, he suffered minor injuries as it says there. Then there's Quincy. But I heard he died in the hospital."

"Died? How many other kids died in the hospital?" Wolfe skimmed the pages looking for reported fatalities.

Jesse took a moment to collect himself. Seeing the pictures brought back gruesome flashbacks to his mind's eye. He backed away from the table, his head throbbing and a heap of anxiety casting over him. He took a deep breath. "I can't tell you."

"What do you mean?"

"I can't stomach it," Rhodes replied.

"Don't worry. I'll read it," said Wolfe.

Wolfe took a moment to skim over the nineteen records. "No other fatalities," he said, "So, we're left with eighteen."

"Which ones sustained facial injuries?" Jesse was looking completely away from the table.

Running back through the files, he pulled out a number of pages containing all male victims suffering burns to their face. "Seven," he blurted out, "Samuel, Brian, Mason, Thadius, Dale, Jonathan, Todd, Forest."

"Addresses?" asked Jesse.

"...All Norman residents, except for one Slaughterville address."

"That wouldn't be it," said Jesse, "Can we run these names through our system, see if we get a match and current address? Maybe we'll even get some updated driver's licenses."

"Wait..." Wolfe bent down closely, looking at the photographs. His eyes nearly escaped their sockets. "Look at this!"

Jesse mustered up the stomach to look down at the table. Wolfe had his finger pointed on one of the pictures, "The facial burns on the six others are closer to their necks, the right side of their faces, or just first-degree, you wouldn't be able to see them after years... look at him."

The Young Detective bent over Wolfe's shoulder. A boy, near the same age as Jesse, the left side of his face, along with forty-five percent of his body suffered third-degree burns. When Jesse saw his face, his gut sank, and something within him knew.

Jesse couldn't help but stare into the man's one dead eye. It was black in the photo, and the one remaining, Jesse could sense, didn't have much soul left to shine through.

"Do you remember him?" Wolfe asked.

"No. Not a bit," Jesse replied. "What's the address?"

"Two-thirteen West Franklin Boulevard," Wolfe stood up from his chair, "It's a long shot, but it's the best we got."

While Buck and O'Massey stayed drooped over in the room, Wolfe and Rhodes headed for the cars. The jet from their office to the house took no more than four minutes with Wolfe's driving. They pulled up to the house on the north side of town. The area was more secluded, but the area was much nicer than the rest of Norman.

The house was two stories with a yard that was bigger than Jesse's old apartment. Two cars, a blue one and a black one, were parked under the awning right next to the side door. The house itself was wooden but painted white with a red trim like the university colors.

Wolfe walked up to the porch while Jesse stayed in the yard, eyeing the place. The windows were all curtained, he couldn't see inside, no one was trying to make their escape through the side door, either.

After another knock, an old, crotchety-looking man opened the door. One eye was squinted all the way shut. He looked Wolfe up and down a bit hesitant to say anything. Wolfe flashed him his badge and began introducing himself.

"I'm Detective Harrison Wolfe," he said, "You own this property?"

"I rent," said the old man with a thick southern accent. "What ya need to know?"

"Rent? How much you pay a month for a place like this?"

"Only 'bout five-hunnered or so dollars; I'm a friend of the family. Most 'time I just give 'em what I got—call it good." said the man.

"What's your name?" Wolfe asked.

"Bill," he replied, "Bill Beck."

"Mr. Beck who owns this property?"

"Oh, well I did belong to my friend, Ryan, I knew him—some odd seven-eight years. He ended up passing not to long ago, His wife, Marrisa owns this lot, now. I ain't seen her well over two years, some odd."

"I'm sorry to hear 'bout that," said Wolfe, "She doin' fine by herself? Where she livin' at, nowadays?"

"Well," said Bill, "Not too long after they started renting this place out to me they ended up findin' a place out in Guymon."

Wolfe turned around and flashed Rhodes a look. Both of them knew their geography quite well—Guymon was in the heart of the Panhandle. It was the epicenter of the Cartel shipping routes. Possibly where Goodman ended up.

"So," said Wolfe, "You ain't heard from any of 'em?"

"Well," Bill began, "I see their son every now and then. Well, not see 'em, really. Whenever he's in town he'll come park his car out here, stay in this shed outback with a little bed. He'll wave, but we don't do much talkin'. He's a bit of a recluse. In his younger years, boy got caught in that church fire 'while back—messed his face up, somethin' good."

"Yeah, I remember that," said Wolfe, "May we see that little shed you were talking about?"

"Well, of course!" said Bill.

Bill took Rhodes and Jesse outback. Behind the house in the backyard a lake engulphed most of the land. Just right of the lake a brown, wooden shed resided. Bill barred open the door to the shack house. From view of the door, all Rhodes and Wolfe could see was a bed, a nightstand, and a heater for when it got cold. Rhodes was the first to walk in, eyeing the place, feeling again the conviction in his gut.

"He's not an any sort of trouble or nutin', is he?" asked Bill, with a worried look about him.

"We're just following up on some leads," assured, Wolfe.

"Well, I guess I'll leave y'all to it, then," he said, "I'll be inside if you need somethin'."

With that, Bill hobbled back toward the house. He went in through the back door nearly tripping over the top step.

Wolfe walked in right after Rhodes, "Guymon!" He said in shock.

"I thought it was a shot in the dark," said Rhodes. "When we get back I'll call the governor's office; we'll leave first thing tomorrow morning."

"You think Bill here can give us an address?" asked Wolfe.

"Perhaps, go in and ask, I'll look around here for a bit."

Wolfe fell out of the shed. Rhodes fell to his knees and looked under the bed. Unfortunately, there was nothing under there for him to find. Wolfe was back within seconds, "He didn't have an address. Anything in here?"

"Nothing," Jesse wiped his brow, "I haven't checked the nightstand, yet."

Wolfe opened the drawer carefully as Jesse made it to his feet. "Oh," Wolfe said opening the drawer.

Rhodes came to see what his fuss was about. Down in the drawer laid a picture. It was the same picture, frame-and-all, that Jesse kept by his bedside. The one of his youth group; most of them put to rest by the fire. The only difference was in pen, someone put in "x" over the kids who'd died. Upon observing the picture closer, York, Lillard, Teal, Smith, Seldom, DeCoupe, and Loggin were all the names crossed out. But over Rhodes a circle was inked around his face.

Jesse turned around and walked out of the shack house. His eyes pointed at the ground. With a sigh, Jesse said,

"We got him."

18

Something Evil Lurks in Guymon

"H-hello? Jesse?"

"Hey! It's good to finally hear your voice."

"I...I'm really happy to hear from you."

"Are you doing okay?"

"Yeah! I'm doing fine. I'm worried about you."

"I'm more worried about you than anything else."

"How's your mom?"

"Good. I called her before I called you. She's seeing her sister at the moment."

"I'm glad...I hope she's happy?"

"She sounded happy."

"Jesse."

"Yeah, Allaura?"

"I love you."

"I...I love you."

"Please say it again."

"I love you."

"Say my name before you say it."

"Allaura...I love you!"

"I love you too, Jesse."

"We have a lead. We're going to No Man's Land."

"The Panhandle? When?"

"Tomorrow."

"You better catch him."

"We will find him."

"Find him for me."

"I'll find him for all of us."

"I love you."

"I love you, too. I'll keep you posted."

It was a good four-and-a-half-hour drive; they began at seven in the morning. They wanted to waste very little time getting there, and staying there, they didn't want to get held up. There only stop came in Woodward, about two hours out, they got gas. Buck prayed to himself under his breath while O'Massey and Wolfe filled the cars. They thought it best to take two vehicles in case one of them got shot at, or something of the sort.

Out there deep in the thick of Oklahoma, it seemed like nothing had changed, Rhodes thought. The farmers were still plowing their fields, corn still grew, cotton still grew, their hay was still rounded up bailed. Out there, it seemed, there was no recession. No scrapping by for an ounce of beans. Still, as it were by that truck stop, Jesse saw smiling faces lurking about, something he hadn't seen in a long time.

He pitied their ignorance. How the world crumbles upon their shoulders, yet, they don't feel a thing. Rhodes wished his life were that. A wife, a few kids, a decent house and the only worry in the world is what's for dinner.

Rhodes stared out across the fields adjacent to the truck stop. They went on for miles. His mind got lost intertwining with the hay fields. Like a hallucination in his head, he dreamed up a big house in the center of that field and a wife dancing in a cotton dress while their children played alongside her. That's all he ever wanted. And there he was chasing down a serial killer in the middle of bumfuck country.

"Come on, Kid," Wolfe patted him on the shoulder, "We don't have all day."

Rhodes hopped back in the car and proceeded the remaining two hours glancing out the window. He hadn't spoken to Allaura since she left. He thought about calling her, but it deemed it safer for her to be left alone. His mother wrote from Georgia every other week. It ripped his heart out with every letter. But he knew the quicker he caught this guy the quicker he'd see his mother again.

The blue sky over the panhandle was slowly succumb to gray and white plumes—a storm was on its way. Rhodes thought it was somewhat poetic. As the Westwind storm rolled in through the sky, an Eastwind storm in the form of four detectives in black carriages came to meet it. Even if their man in Guymon, Oklahoma turned out not to be their guy, they meant business. They would have their man sooner or later.

The four men parked their cars on the main road through town. From their demeanor and poise, the locals noticed them quick. With heads down, locked on their boots, they kept about their business.

Rhodes and the others rushed out of their cars and met together on the sidewalk in front of a bar. "Everyone keep it calm. From what I take it, everyone here knows everyone else. Someone knows who he is." Wolfe walked into the bar.

Buck walked in behind him. As Rhodes was falling in line behind him, O'Massey tugged his shoulder back. "Talk to me for a sec," he said.

"What do you need?" Rhodes said with a stern tone.

"Buck's still working on those scriptures our guy left on the Crawford girl's bed. He can't make heads or tails of it." said Shane.

"It's been two weeks," said Rhodes, "She has to be dead at this point, I'm sure."

"He didn't want me mentioning it," Shane said, "but I must tell you straight like I told Wolfe. They found cancer in one of his kidneys—thing's the size of a grapefruit."

"Jesus," Rhodes cried. "He tell his wife, yet?"

"Juanita knows," he said, "I know you ain't got much of a heart, but he believes God's gonna get him through it like he got you through that shit in P.V."

"Sad to think," said Jesse, "God works his miracles on the wrong people."

"How did you survive all that, anyway? I never asked you."

"I just told you: God wastes his miracles on the wrong people."

Jesse walked into the bar. Mostly the people inside were just scared civilians trying to drown their sorrows in a cold beer, a chunk of them were Cartel members praying off the local business for free booze. He could tell which were Cartel-protected by their arrogant happiness—locals just kept to themselves trying not to step on the wrong toes.

Wolfe was at the bar ordering a bottle, Buck asked for water. When the bartender, a woman well past forty and a tattoo of all her children's names woven into a rose on her left shoulder, brought back their drinks, Wolfe had the photo ready.

"You seen him?" Wolfe asked.

The woman looked at the picture for a flash, "Boy's lived in this town for almost ten years. Why'd I tell you pigs where he's at? Gonna give him more trouble than he's already had in his lifetime?"

"We just want to talk to him. He isn't under arrest...at this time."

"Ion' care 'bout him too much. Always sits in the corner—scares the people who come in. No people means no tips. No tips means no money. No money means I can't feed my four kids. Their daddy's ain't providing. Their daddys all work at the biodiesel plant across town. They ain't paying them what they used to. Oh, well, anyway, He lives out on the outskirts west of town. Kinda wooded area—off the main road. Can't miss it if you're looking for it."

"Thank you," said Wolfe, "You've been helpful." As Jesse was approaching the bar, Buck and Wolfe walked away leaving the beer and water dripping cold.

"Pay the women, there, Kid," said Wofle, "make sure to tip her well. She has kids."

Buck let out a hardy chuckle. Rhodes threw down a fifty-dollar bill and followed the other detectives out of the bar.

The two cars sped out as if they were flying out of hell. The trip north didn't take more than a minute. The backroad was aligned with trees shrouded by more trees. The serenity and lush of it all, it put chills down their backs.

After five miles, they'd reached a gravel road on the left—they couldn't see a house from where they turned in, so they kept going. Eventually they came up on a double-wide trailer on cinder blocks with sheds and shacks laid in behind the main house. Across the yard, between the trees, burned trash piles mounted up like mole hills. They drove up on the house slowly, hoping not to alarm anyone who happened to be lurking about.

The musk in the air was thick. The scent of burnt plastic and rot invaded their nostrils. It was so potent standing there in the yard they had to cover their mouths and noses. It got to Shane the worst; he started gagging, threatening to vomit.

They approached the porch, stepping up onto the old, wooden, tiles. They creaked underneath them, especially Buck.

The front door was nothing more than a screen door. Clearly, all four of them could see through into the living room. Where there had previously been a door was ripped from its hinges and discarded. Wolfe peered through the screen looking into the house. He could see the main living space was barren of furniture and replaced with various trash.

Rhodes was to his right peering in the opposite side. He got a better view of the kitchen, which was also kept poorly. Dishes laced with grime and roaches overloaded the sink. The "white" countertops were every color except white. Cabinets had been ripped off the wall partially and house broken plates and Tupperware.

"Should we go around back?" Shane asked Wolfe in a hushed voice.

"No," said Wolfe. "Stay close."

"Wolfe..." Rhodes' voice cracked a little, "look there in the back room."

Following the point of Jesse's finger, Wolfe glanced into the first door on the left down the back hall. The door was ajar. A glimpse of the bed was all they needed. They could see the outlining of a person tucked in under the comforter. Their hand, and nothing else, was visible.

Rhodes gave a slight tap to the screen door. "Police department," he gave a yell.

The hand didn't move its position. Rhodes didn't bother to tap the screen again. Retrieving his gun, he pressed down on the little handle and swung the door open slowly so it wouldn't squeal.

Wolfe fell in behind, then Shane, then Buck. The closer they got to the back room, the better they could tell...

"Oh, shit..." muttered Wolfe.

The hand showing through the door was the color of a stormy sky. Maggots had already intertwined into the fingers and up the decayed skin. The scent got thicker with every advancement. With the base of his gun Rhodes pushed open the door. The person on the bed was nearly skeletonized. Black and gray decay fermented on the once white sheets.

Rhodes and Wolfe jumped back pointing their guns into the room. When the door swung wide open, to their surprise, a second body hung from the ceiling at the foot of the bed. The body was dangling from its neck like the Beaumont Girls.

Maggots and other larvae squirmed from the hanging body's eyelids and fell to the floor. The ground was crawling with the miscreants. So much decay riddled the room it withered into the walls. At the sight and smell all the detectives had the overwhelming urge to lose their lunch.

Buck darted around the corner; his senses couldn't handle the aroma. Thirty-plus years on the job still doesn't prepare you for certain things.

"Told you not to eat all those snacks in the car," Shane grunted.

Wolfe entered the room behind Rhodes. O'Massey stayed on the outside looking in also keeping an eye on

Buck who was still recuperating. The Young Detective pulled a handkerchief from his coat pocket. He patted the pockets of the body hanging from the ceiling. In the right-front, he felt a square object protruding from the fabric. He reached in and pulled out the man's wallet. Wolfe was approaching the woman on the bed as he took notice of the wallet in Jesse's hand. His face dropped, "I know that wallet."

There wasn't anything particular about the wallet. Just a brown leather wallet that had been withered from time and longevity of its use. Rhodes unfolded the flaps. On the left side was a police badge dispersed by the Norman Police Department. On the right was the slip which showed the man's I.D.

"Oh my god…" Rhodes gawked at the name displayed next to the picture on the identification card. He'd never seen the man's face before, but the name was enough.

"It's him, isn't it?" Wolfe's voice cracked, his eyes slumped more than his face.

"I-It's Goodman." Rhodes looked up from the wallet; he couldn't believe it. The pit in his stomach turned into a rock.

"Fuck," Wolfe grumbled. He could barely look up to see his friend of thirty or more years—missing—finally found. Maggot-filled, decayed, and hung by the neck.

O'Massey shared in his grief. But unlike Wolfe, he couldn't remove his eye from the horrid scene. He didn't speak a word, but the tears that rolled off his cheeks told enough. The years hadn't made him, Wolfe, or Buck any softer. But that was their friend. In a job where it was theirs to clean up the shit after it been dumped, the world was supposed to happen to everyone else…but not them.

"Don't tell me…" Buck hurled from the living room.

"We'll have to call the Governor's office—we need to call this in." Rhodes spoke in a low voice.

"I promised Shannon I would find him. I'd bring him home…not like this." Wolfe cried out.

"Why would he just leave them here?" Shane whimpered.

Rhodes stared horridly at the bodies; he was the only detective that could. The rope looked fresher than the bodies would dictate. Between the grime and muck of decay, bits of dirt showed present, clinging to the bodies.

"He didn't just leave them here," said Rhodes, "he unburied them and displayed them for us."

"We'll who the fuck is she?" Wolfe exclaimed.

"Look at the picture on the nightstand," demanded Rhodes, "it's got to be his mother."

God's Detective, "Buck" Jordan feel ill across the trashed living room. Behind him was the kitchen and the kitchen door which led out to the side yard under the awning. From the cornered windows of the door, the feral killer Jonathan Davis eyed him through the glass. The grin on his face brought a darker mystique to his piercing, dead eyes. His charred skin was covered in dirt from digging the bodies up from the yards of the compound. His eyes were locked on Buck.

Tap, tap, tap...

His grin widened as his finger punched the glass to lure Buck's attention.

Buck turned around from a hunched over position. At first he didn't see where the tapping was coming from. He looked around the corner into the kitchen—saw nothing—nearly went back down the hall with the others until again...

Tap, tap, tap, tap...

God's Detective nearly stepped back into his own vomit. He, "Buck" Jordan, was locking eyes with the killer. The top left half of his face was melted away along with most of his lips. Even though they were nearly gone, Buck could see he was grinning menacingly at him.

"Hey! Hey! Oh my—you—stop!" Buck cried out beginning his sprint towards the side door.

"Buck? Aye, what's going on?" Rhodes started for the living room. O'Massey and Wolfe directly behind him; all guns drawn.

Davis ran to his right out of view of Buck. Buck took his hands and violently tried to open the door. After realizing it was unlocked, he twisted the notch and swung the door open with haste.

"He was right there—I saw him!" Buck called out.

"Buck--WAIT!" Wolfe held his hand out, "STOP!"

Buck didn't listen. He should've listened...

Just under the side door were two concrete steps that led down under the awning. Under the last step, atop the gravel driveway, various pieces of dead grass and sticks were leveled out in a decent-sized pile. Buck, with all his weight, stepped down right onto the center of the pile with one foot. With the cunning snap of the mechanism, the bear trap which hid underneath the pile jumped up and dug its ridged points into the meat of Buck's calf. He cried out, as he tried to step out of it the fangs only dug deeper. "GOD!" he cried out.

At the end of the gravel road behind the house, that beige car was sitting there, engine roaring. Davis, no hesitation, pressed the pedal all the way down to the padding; the tires squawled. The car lunged forward; Buck saw the car coming right at him. He had only a second to react—Buck, bouncing off his free leg, tried to make a last-minute effort to get back on the steps. He fell forward, but he was too obtuse of a man to fully steer clear of the vehicle. The grill of the car caught his on the side of his gut and propelled him forward throwing him against the side of the house. He fell over, his face buried in the gravel.

Rhodes, Wolfe, and O'Massey rushed from the door, leaping onto the naked gravel in case there was another bear trap. There wasn't a single bullet left in any of their clips when they unloaded them at the retreating car. The back windshield exploded; the sound of gunfire cut through the wind. Davis drove with his head buried between the center console and the passenger's seat. He knew when he'd hit the main road whenever the feel of the terrain impacted the car's wheels. Once the front wheels hit paydirt, he cut his wheels right and by then he had an army of trees to cover his escape.

"SHIT!" Wolfe exclaimed with an empty clip.

O'Massey knelt down by his friend. Buck's eyes were closed, jaw open. Wolfe checked for a pulse; he couldn't feel one in his neck, so he checked his wrist.

"He's alive," Wolfe cried out pressing his pulse.

Rhodes looked over Buck like a deer in headlights. Buck's suit was ripped where he was impacted by the car, red spilled out over the cloth and gravel. He got on his knees and started applying pressure to the open wound.

"We have to get him out of here—get on a phone!" Rhodes said.

"There's no reception out here, we'll have to drive him. Get him in the car!" O'Massey picked up Buck under his shoulder blades.

"We can't move him," said Rhodes.

"We can't just leave him here," Wolfe retorted.

Rhodes grabbed him by the legs while Wolfe reached under him trying to hoist him up at the back. On Shane's count of three, they grunted and cried trying to move the three-hundred-sixty pounds of dead weight. Buck screamed in agony, blood dripped down his side, his skin turned an alarming pale. The noises he made after were like a wounded animal: heavy breathing and gasping for every morsel of air.

"Wolfe, get the door!" Shane grunted, his face red, dripping with sweat.

Wolfe let go of Buck and raced to the back door of one of the black vehicles. He swung the back door open as O'Massey was backing into it.

"Gah--ah!" Buck cried out reaching for his side where he was struck.

Rhodes gasped out as well nearly dropping his legs. "My, God—Fuck!" he gasped.

Buck's intestines herniated then broke through the open wound. A string of guts fell out of him touching the gravel road. O'Massey maneuvered getting his top half in the back of the car. His body tensed up in horror seeing his insides poured out.

Rhodes pushed him in the vehicle as gently as he could. He then ripped off his coat and, with some reluctance, picked up his entrails and pushed them back inside them applying pressure over the open wound. Wolfe darted around the car into the driver's seat. O'Massey climbed in the passenger's while Rhodes stayed in the back with him holding the wound.

Wolfe soared off the compound hitting the turn at nearly fifty miles an hour. "Where the fuck is the hospital?" Wolfe shouted.

"Take me back to Norman," Buck mutters, his face turning pale.

Once he made it back to the main road blue H road signs directed their path. Buck moaned at every sudden stop or jolt of the car. They pulled up to Guymon General within minutes.

Nurses trotted out of the automatic doors to meet the detectives. Wolfe stormed out of the car in a frantic panic.

"N-n-n—" Buck stuttered trying to raise his hand.

Wolfe darted and approached the two women

"I need a wheelchair—now!" Wolfe cried at them. "That man's a detective, he's dying!"

Shane got out and opened the door Buck was leaning his head against, "N-n-n..." he continued.

Rhodes readied himself to get his legs again. Wolfe was surprised the two men didn't share in his alertness to get Buck inside the E.R. The nurses looked at the four men in realization and backed away.

"Hey..." Wolfe said, "Help him!"

"Sorry, sir, Governor's orders," said one of the nurses.

"THAT MAN IS DYING—PLEASE!"

"N-n...Norman!" Buck finished.

The nurses walked back inside and didn't look back.

Wolfe's face turned from aggressive to helpless. His eyes drooped, turned soggy, as he put his hands up and backed up towards the car.

"What?" Shane winced, having Buck by the shoulders.

"They're not gonna help us." said Wolfe in a grumble. "We have to get him to Woodward!"

Wolfe jumped back in the car. Shane pressed Buck forward then slammed the door and raced back around. Wolfe sped off slapping the steering wheel and screaming out in anger.

"Norman..." Buck grumbled out.

"Don't worry, Buck," we're getting you some help, just hold on!" said Rhodes.

"I ain't... I ain't going to no hospital that isn't in Norman."

"Buck, we don't have time for all that, now!" Wolfe yelled back at him pressed the gas.

"I'm...I'm already dying, Harris...Take me back to Norman so I can see my Juanita one last time."

Wolfe looked down. His eyes teared up as the words he was trying to speak were ripped away by the tightness in his throat. O'Massey covered his mouth and hunched over placing his head on the dashboard.

Not a word was spoken on that four-hour trip back to Norman...

19

Spirit Come

Buck lingered on all the way to Norman Health Plex. There wasn't much fight left in him after that. Wolfe made sure to call his wife well before their arrival; as well as alerting the hospital. It was at around eleven thirty when Buck's body finally gave out. The internal damages, along with the cancer, had done their work. Juanita was right by him the entire time. Wolfe and Shane were able to be with him in those final moments, too. Rhodes kept to himself outside the I.C.U.

The funeral was at his church in Lexington. The detectives sat front row in their black suits. A hundred or so of the town's folk attended the service. After hearing of the tragedy on the news, as well as Buck being a leading member in their community, tears shed throughout. Rhodes never seen a man so mourned. Townsfolk, families, members of his church, children and adults alike—Spurgeon "Buck" Jordan was a man beloved. He didn't deserve his fate.

Wolfe and O'Massey stayed stone-faced, along with Rhodes. After the pastor gave his eulogy, they opened the casket and allowed people to say their last goodbyes. The cries got even louder. As if seeing his body lying there, at rest, made it all the more real.

Buck was buried east of Lexington in a small graveyard surrounded by open pastures. Perhaps his soul could wonder them alongside the almighty. Or perhaps his soul would linger in the caves of darkness that all things go back to. They'd have no way of knowing.

Within the following days the name and face of Jonathan Davis was on every news outlet across The Plains. The authorities seized the compound in Guymon. Possessions along with the bodies were all apprehended and brought back to Norman. The land was dug up for more bodies, potentially. All the remains that were found were animal carcasses. The holes where Goodman and Mrs. Davis were buried not even fifteen yards from the back of the house. He didn't even bother to refill the holes.

Wolfe and O'Massey spoke to the coroner as Goodman's body laid on a metal table. They were informed his cause of death was a bullet to the spine. They both had the displeasure of informing Goodman's late wife. They were just as broken as she was. The fucker got two of their friends.

Rhodes oversaw the compiling of evidence brought into their headquarters. It was all sorted, listed and put in the system all later to be used against Jonathan when they caught him. It was only a matter of time.

"...Item number fifty-three," said a cop placing another piece from the Guymon House on the gathering of tables, "pendent; blood residue along the cross. Item number fifty-four: GPS coordinates tracking device; destroyed. Item number fifty-five: Family photo of the Davis family; faces of the mother and father burnt out; glass shattered..."

"Detective Rhodes," said a woman's voice, poking her head into the board room office, "You have a call waiting on line one—says it's your brother."

Rhodes looked up, confused at the woman, "I don't have a brother."

The woman bent her head down and shrugged. She poked her head out of the room and walked away. The room suddenly got quiet, the cops all eyeing Rhodes. "Lieutenant," Rhodes gasped, "trace this call."

"On it, Detective," the Lieutenant left the room with a sergeant. The other cops in the room stayed, shrills up their backs. Rhodes picked up the landline and pressed the button for line one.

"Hello." said Rhodes.

There was silence before the person on the other line chose to respond. Rhodes could hear the noise of the person shuffling around, then finally a reply, "We are brothers. Our bonds our burned on our sleeves. Also a good chunk of my face."

"My backs pretty fucked up—didn't get off too easy." Rhodes replied.

The man on the other line chuckled, "Yeah, I know."

"I knew you were crazy. But calling me at my office? You got some nerve."

"Right. I got to give it to you, you're pretty smart for figuring all this stuff out. I always figure I have more time, then here you are to remind me otherwise. You're smarter than I remember. But eventually I would've made you smarten up, real quick."

"You're caught, Jonathan. Turn yourself in before things get messier." Rhodes grunted.

"You think it matters if people know who I am? I could've told you who I was in a letter and save you the trip to no man's land...but then I would have one less cop on my count."

"Is that right?" Rhodes scoffed, "What's the move, now? There's no way you can keep this going much longer. We're on your tail."

"I've still killed more people than you've saved. I'd say I'm better at my job than you are yours."

"You got jokes, eh?" Rhodes turned away from the cops, "I don't have jokes, Jonathan. All I have to say is I'm going to put you in a cage like the peasant you are. If I don't kill you first."

"Big words, Jesse. Funny, I didn't think you cared about anyone else at all. I guess only your girls, is that it? I have a question: How'd I know you'd be coming to my house? I didn't just dig up the detective and my bitch mom for no good reason."

"You tell me."

"Well, guess you have a lot to learn. Funny to note how you don't know how sloppy you are until after you've slopped up."

"You're not as smart as you think you are, Jonathan." Rhodes ripped at him.

"Neither are you. Have you 'considered the scriptures'?"

"Where is Kaytlynn? Is she still alive?"

"No. I don't like letting women linger on—the gentleman in me."

"Where is she? Tell me?"

The two cops stormed back in the room. The Lieutenant had a piece of paper in his hand. He slapped it on the desk in front of Rhodes.

"It was a little birthday present for you. I know Buck was still trying to decipher my hidden meaning and I'm feeling generous."

"Jonathan...what'd you do?"

"Come get it, sweetheart."

The static made a clicking sound when Jonathan hung up the phone. "We get him?" asked Rhodes to the Lieutenant.

The lieutenant looked down at his radar. With pungent rage he struck the table, "We didn't get him!"

The room shared in an dissatisfied groan. Curses and failed arms exchanged throughout. None were louder than Rhodes, "FUCK!" the proclamation echoed across the floor.

Rain pitter-pattered on the windows. Light rumbles warned the rolling sky. A gray hue filled the room, and suddenly all was quiet to the young detective. *What's there to consider,* he thought.

Trying to tap into the mind of a serial killer was no easy task, but Rhodes had to give it a shot. He'd remembered Buck hovering over the scriptures for hours; breaking down each word in them from multiple translations. *Perhaps,* Rhodes thought, *Davis knew I'd give the task to him. Maybe the preacher would've considered the scriptures too much.*

"Get me a copy of the scriptures in the Crawford note—Now!" Rhodes demanded.

A woman ran out of the room and quickly back in with a yellow file in her hand. Rhodes snatched it from her and opened it. He noted, firstly, how the scriptures were arrayed in the note: A line on the left side of the page, and a line on the right side. Two pillars of scripture.

They must be split apart for a reason, Rhodes thought.

Murmurs begin to sprinkle around the room like the rain outside. "QUIET!" Rhodes yelled.

Scriptures...books, chapters, verses...perhaps that isn't what matters...

Rhodes found a notepad and stroked each digit onto the yellow page corresponding with its column. *Eight digits a piece...*

"I got it!"

"Wha-what?" asked a sergeant.

"It's not the scriptures..."

Rhodes stomped out of the room. Wolfe and O'Massey were beside themselves by Buck's desk pouring beer over the desktop. The emotions were still fresh for them. "Wolfe!" Rhodes broke their silence.

The cops in the war room migrated out to the main floor. Wolfe looked up, disgruntled. With a cocky smirk on his face, Rhodes headed out the door, the cops following.

"They're coordinates!" cried Rhodes.

The sudden realization hit them like semi. Wolfe and O'Massey exchanged looks, their perplexed expressions in sync. Wolfe ran back to his office and grabbed his coat, Shane grabbing his shoulder holster off his desk and the detectives made their way out of the Norman Police Department.

20

Find Me

What made Oklahoma so unique was the simplicity of it all. The hills that expanded into mountain ranges, the trees that swayed with the wind that made the plains dance. The air in their lungs was the same breath the Indians sang with. The simplicity of life there gave that region life. Simplicity has its setbacks. It's as easy to get lost out here as it is a concrete jungle. And that's exactly what happened to Kaytlynn Crawford.

 Detective Jesse Rhodes led the squad cars out into the pasture lands just north of town. The No Man's Land between Norman and Oklahoma City consisted of cow fields, plots, private property, and untouched lands filled with lakes and untamed terrain. All that surrounded Norman was Cow Country. To this dismay, a lot more than a leisurely stroll awaited the young detective.

 Three miles down a back road and a few uncertain winds in the road, Rhodes jolted from his car and leaped over a barb wire fence. The entirety of the Norman Police force at his back. Wolfe and O'Massey called out to him, "Rhodes! Rhodes slow down!" But there was no slowing him down.

 The rain picked up through the field. With a mighty rumble the plains shook while thunder rolled. Lightning cascaded across the sky and along the horizon like a painter's fatal brush stroke. The wind shook them around like a playground bully wanting lunch money.

 Rhodes spit rainwater out as it fell from his brow to his lips. Ahead of him there was a divot in the field. It was a pond in a previous life that had since dried up. A canyon that was once a stream branched out west of the crater. In the very center of the dried pond...Rhodes found her lying flat on her back.

Her appendages were spread out; her arms above her head and her legs opened at shoulder length. Rhodes slid down into the crater and loomed over top of her.

Crawford had endured most of her burns across her arms and unfortunately the right side of her neck and face. They weren't as severe as Davis' but at the sight of them it was apparent. He'd made sure to tilt her head to lay on its left, showing her perfect imperfections up to the heavens to see, and for Detective Rhodes to find. As if to say, *this is who you are.*

The battalion had caught up with him. Wolfe and O'Massey stood over the dried pond with rain puddling around her. She sunk as the dirt turned into mud and the stench traveled through the air.

Wolfe clinched his fists while the veins in his neck and brow popped out. His teeth gritted; he couldn't help looking down at the girl, instead looking out into the wooded area of the field.

O'Massey trembled through the shivered from the chilled rain. He couldn't take his eyes off the scene. He'd seen things like this before, and sometimes worse. Thirty years would make a man grow numb to whole ordeal. But the crass detective felt a gumption in his belly; a fever. His heart pounded through his chest and his skin felt light and cold. His eyes bugged and his pupils shook, as if he wanted to look away, but simply couldn't.

The thunder rolled over the young detective and the Crawford girl. He looked down at her with a pale stare. She'd been one of many, but one too many. She didn't have to die, yet there she was. When they were teens, Jesse remembered, she was an equestrian. She belonged out here in these fields on bare horseback letting the wind blow through her brown hair and soothing her tan, Sunkist skin like her ancestors before her. Yet, here she lay, half-decayed and sinking into mud. The thunder rolled again, her hair matted and falling off her scalp. The life that resonated behind the brown wells she saw God's creation through told more than the horrid tale of her heartbreaking end. The thunder rolled, and the lightning struck the field, and Jesse Rhodes screamed to the heavens as if to tell God: *Look at her! Are you proud?*

Rhodes looked back down at the Crawford girl, his eyes bawling. A slip of paper latched to her chest. The words were leaky from the rain but still clear to read.

"Find me where Adam met Eve"

Wolfe and O'Massey made their way into the pond with mud-covered pant legs and boots. Wolfe looked down and read the note, as did O'Massey.

"What does it mean?" Wolfe looked to Rhodes.

With a staggered breath, Rhodes replied, "I don't know."

21

Where Adam Met Eve

The trio of detectives took their notes and were back at the Norman Police Headquarters before nightfall. The police on scene and crime cleaners still lingered on as news crews had alerted the public of another Silver-Faced Ripper attack.

The news report played on floor four. The family was notified by O'Massey. Each phone call to the next-of-kin never got easier. He routinely fumbled his words, and his offers of condolences were vain, nonetheless.

Rhodes and Wolfe lingered about going back and forth between desks and rooms; contemplating. The note's message rung over and over; even written across the wall. Their brain was almost hindered from coming up with a solution.

"The Garden..." Wolfe muttered, "The Gardens in O-K-C? No..."

That was the only idea muttered that night. As if stunned exhaustion overwhelmed them. Rhodes contemplated over Buck's old Bible. It was opened to Genesis. The pages were highlighted heavily and riddled with notes; Rhodes could barely read the small print. So decorated with personal interpretations.

Shane walked into the room and stood in the doorway. Wolfe and Rhodes looked up at him waiting for him to say something. His pale face flushed red. He scratched the bald spot on his head and panted. "Please tell me y-you figured it out?"

"Not yet, Shane," said Wolfe, "Help us brainstorm."

Shane pressed his forearms against the doorframe, his torso drooped, and his legs bent.

"'You okay?" Rhodes stood up looking down at Shane who was almost on his knees.

"I worked with Buck for nearly thirty years. He always told me *praying* was his answer to everything. Whenever it got too tough, he'd always pray...and the Lord would see him through. Not once have I ever prayed; he never broke me to pray. I guess everyone prays, eventually..."

"Shane?" Wolfe took a step towards him.

Shane fumbled inside his coat for a moment. He dropped to his knees and closed his eyes, his head tilted to the ceiling.

"*...See me to the gates.*"

Shane pulled his gun from inside his coat and rose it to his head. "NO!" Rhodes yelled, clearing the table to run to him.

Wolfe sprang forward and tackled Shane forcing him to fall on his back. Wolfe made it to his knees and grabbed Shane's wrist to gain control of the gun. "LET ME DO IT!" Shane yelled.

Rhodes knelt down with force onto Shane's free arm then double-gripped his other wrist. Shane cried out as Wolfe managed to pry the gun from his hand. He stood up while Rhodes kept him pinned and unloaded the pistol.

"Taking! Taking! They all just take! Let me take...let me take for once!"

Wolfe broke down the gun, putting the muzzle in his pocket and throwing the other half across the floor. He stared down as Shane struggled with Rhodes; crying, weak from pity.

"I can't take it. I'm drowning, Harrison," Shane cried out. "I want it to end."

Rhodes felt it unnecessary to keep O'Massey pinned down. He'd quit struggling. His body trembled as his soul cried out. The tears poured and landed on the carpet.

"Take him to a holding cell," suggested Rhodes.

Wolfe brought O'Massey to his feet by his shoulders. Shane couldn't stand straight up. He whimpered more as Wolfe put him on the elevator.

"I'll stay with him," Wolfe said as the elevator door met.

Rhodes grew numb looking at his reflection in the elevator door. He walked back to his desk looking at the pieces of metal and led scattered across the floor.

...

The Young Detective wasn't too keen on counting his blessings. But Shane's upheaval is just what he needed in that moment. If there was ever a divine time for a mental breakdown, that was that exact moment. Jesse had down exactly what Jonathan Davis meant the second he'd read the message; he couldn't let the others know. If they'd figured it out, it would've been over. But Jesse wasn't going to let it end on Davis's terms. This was going to end the way Rhodes envisioned.

"Back to Genesis," Rhodes checked the clip of his pistol before placing it back inside the gun, "let's go."

On the outskirts of the southeast side of town were the ruins of a church that burned down long ago. Rhodes hadn't been back there since that day. He swore never to go see it again. But as fate would have it, Rhodes had a ripper to catch.

Before he left, he wrote a note and left it on the desk. Perhaps a note to whomever found it first. More than likely Wolfe. Maybe things were meant to come full circle for the young detective. Through all the near-death experiences, maybe Jesse was always met to meet God there—to see the gates himself like Buck did.

The distance wasn't far; maybe a six-minute drive. It was exactly how he left it all those years ago. Rhodes peaked over the steering wheel and just gawked a moment. Rain on the windshield blurred his view, but the nerves that crept into his soul at the sight of it turned his senses into prey. He took steady breaths. "I will not die here!" he proclaimed.

Jesse stepped out of the car and ripped the gun from his holster. He walked with heavy steps, rain and gravel jumping with every stomp. "I will not die here!"

Rhodes pounded his chest. He made it to the front door which had long been removed from its hinges; he stepped over it. He entered the sanctuary, the charred pews still aligned facing the pulpit. He walked to the very center of the room, "I will not die here! JONATHAN!" the echos clashed to the roll of thunder.

The reverberation was all he heard. Blue flashes illuminated the church in the split blink of an eye. Rhodes' eyes widened. He circled around waiting for the predator to strike. Rhodes faced the pulpit. Just as he was about to proceed forward, a rumble of thunder, then the boast snap of lightning, Rhodes fell forward.

Dazed, he rolled to his back and faced the entrance, The Melted-Face Ripper stood over him. Covered in mud and rain; his mask was in his hand, he held it through the eye slits. His breaths turned into exaggerated grunts with a slight wheeze on the end.

"You were stupid to come alone," said Davis.

Rhodes fired three shots; he had twenty. Davis ran and leaped behind some pews and then fell quiet under the rain. Rhodes maneuvered and found a hiding place of his own. He saw something move across from him on the ladder side; he shot but to no avail.

"You'll only make it out of here alive if I allow it!" Davis's rasp reverberated through the scorched sanctuary.

Rhodes stayed poised. He scanned through the darkened haze, light drizzles of rain seeping through the holes in the ceiling. He waited for the rumbles, then the almost immediate flash of blue light. The thunder rolled, the lightning struck—Rhodes caught eye of Davis knelt in the third row. He let off two shots which embedded into the charred wood.

Davis crept back into a shadow as Rhodes advanced to the opposite section of pews. "When I kill you, it won't be slowly," Davis lowered the octaves in his voice.

Rhodes popped his head over the pews. He scarcely let his breath escape. He stared out into the sections trying to catch a glimpse of a silhouette. With the illumination of a blue flash, Rhodes staggered back. Davis crept up on his side and tackled him to the ground. Rhodes managed to keep hold of his weapon, but before he could regain himself enough to shoot, Davis crept back into another hiding spot.

"Hehehe," he howled, "This is how they *all* died."

Rhodes stood back into the center aisle. He felt like he was being toyed with—like the prey being pawed at before being consumed. "Face me like a man!" Rhodes lost his composure.

"I will say...you died the least cowardly."

Rhodes heard the shuffling of feet pattering towards him from behind. He turned around; the silhouette shown at the steps of the pulpit. Davis fell into the front row with a loud clash to follow. Rhodes ran down, gun forward. He stepped into a small red puddle.

Lightning struck. The silver mask laid at Rhodes' feet, but there was no melt-face to go along with it. Rhodes looked around and saw nothing, but he knew he had a wounded predator. "Come out!" Rhodes shouted. He stood under a hole in the ceiling, the moonlight illuminating his position. It was a grave mistake.

Davis jolted his body into Rhodes' ribcage. They fell onto the steps of the altar, Jonathan with the upper hand. The Ripper threw punches with his right hand as he had Rhodes' left arm hooked under him; the gun was pointed out behind him. Blood gushed from his right bicep. Every blow sent a shockwave of pain into the open wound back down to his fingertips. The killer screamed and grunted with aggression and poise flooding out of him. He then grabbed Rhodes' wrist and bit down on his pulse. Rhodes screamed, his teeth piercing through the flesh. His closed hand opened and released grip of the gun.

Rhodes pushed forward pounding his elbow into Jonathan's eye. Jonathan unlatched his jaw and Rhodes pulled away his wrist. The gun was invisible in the stormy moonlight. Rhodes cocked his head back and bluntly collided foreheads with the Ripper. Davis put his hands up trying to go for Rhodes' eyes but Rhodes was quick to evade. The young detective pressed his thumbs into the center of Davis's neck.

"I... will not...die here!" Rhodes proclaimed.

Davis grabbed Rhodes by the forearms trying to break his hold. Rhodes was stronger than him. Davis unlatched his grip and started reaching out for anything he could get his hands on. His right hand found his metal mask near the pool of blood. With a swift strike, he bludgeoned the young detective's temple. He caught him with the top corner of the mask which he'd sharpened on purpose. The tip pierced his skin. He fell sideways, the blood dripping into his mouth.

Davis staggered to his knees gasping. His wheezes and pants turned subtlety into laughter. "Jesse," he whispered, "we *all* died here. You just never realized it." he then knelt on top of Rhodes, mask still in hand, "You're going to learn today, boy."

The Ripper beat Rhodes' head in some more. He'd lost so much blood; he couldn't muster the strength to fight back. Davis crashed the mask into his head seven more times, then threw the mask away like useless trash. He screamed to the heavens as if God favored him to win. The Ripper smiled through melted flesh and pouring rain.

Suddenly a light shined through the holes in the roof. And not just through the holes in the roof, light came from outside as well.

"NORMAN POLICE WE HAVE THE PLACE SURROUNDED!" a voice echoed on a megaphone.

Davis lowered his hands and looked up, then looked down the aisle. "It's over...it's finally over."

Rhodes shot up like a rushing wind. He wrapped his legs around Jonathan's waist then grabbed his wrist and swung his own arm behind his back. With his free arm he grabbed his arm forearm locking Davis in an arm lock. Rhodes screamed, blood and phlegm flying from his mouth. Davis shouted out; right where the bullet lodged into his skin is where the bone snapped in Rhodes' grip.

The young detective pushed the Ripper off him, landing on his broken arm. Jesse reached for his gun, found it in the darkness and proclaimed, "Jonathan Davis," he stood over him, "you're under arrest!"

22

The Girl in the Chair

Harrison Wolfe stood ahead of a barricade of police vehicles. A helicopter illuminated the perimeter around the abandoned church in case Jonathan Davis decided to make a break for it. He had a megaphone in his hand, "Davis... come on out!" He paused a moment. "Rhodes, you in there?" he said less authority in his voice and more concern.

The broken entrance door flew from the frame. The cops poised their weapons. Bloody face and all, Detective Jesse Rhodes dragged a cuffed serial killer out by the broken arm. Davis was curled in a ball, mumbling to himself—making it as hard as he could for Rhodes to pull him out of there.

Relief flushed over Wolfe and the rest of the police force. Two cops ran out as Rhodes dropped the Ripper on the gravel and limped to Wolfe like. "I got your note!" said Wolfe.

"We...we got him. We got the bastard." Rhodes spoke through heavy exhalation.

"Genesis? Moreso Revelations." Wolfe patted Rhodes on the shoulder with a smile.

The cops dragged Davis into the back of a cruiser. "My arm is broken. I need medical attention." Davis voice was expressionless; no grunts of pain or discomfort.

"Tell someone who gives a shit!" said the cop, throwing him into the back of the police van and slamming the door.

"I'll follow them back to headquarters," said Rhodes.

"I'll clean this place up, don't worry about a thing, Rhodes. Get what you can out of him!"

Rhodes reached out to Wolfe. He grabbed the handkerchief in his breast pocket and started wiping the blood from his face. "You alright?" asked Wolfe.

"Never better," replied Rhodes, "see you at headquarters."

Rhodes hopped back in his car and sped down to headquarters behind the police van—sirens blaring. They booked Davis and threw him in a metal room with a glass one-way window on the back wall. Rhodes watched him for the better part of an hour.

Jonathan Davis sat calmly in his chair. His head drooped over the table, arms still cuffed behind his back. The Ripper didn't make a sound. Rhodes turned the corner and walked into the room; Davis still quiet.

"How's the arm?" asked Rhodes, trying to sound concerned but even his motives were to taunt.

Jonathan had no answer. He didn't even tilt his head or adjust his arm to bring comfort to it.

"How was the drive here? Were the pigs kind to you?"

Jonathan Davis had no answer, again.

Rhodes came around to the front of the table. He placed his hands down where Jonathan could see them, his shadow cast over the back of his neck. "Does it all feel for nothing, Jonathan?"

"You think you've won, don't you, Jesse?" Jonathan finally looked up at Rhodes with a smirk on his face.

This answer threw Rhodes off. He adjusted his posture, his back straight and his knees locked. "You weren't going to shake us for long, Davis," he said.

"That's not what I asked," said Jonathan. "Do you *think* you've won?"

"No." Rhodes answered with honesty. "But I know you're better behind bars which is exactly where you'll be."

"That's a good answer. A stoic answer." Jonathan grumbled, hunching back over the table.

"Why did you do all of this, Jonathan?"

"After the fire, my mom moved me to Guymon. She isolated me, didn't let me play with the other kids anymore. They said out of everyone—everyone who survived—I'd sustained the worst injuries. Half your face melted; that's pretty tough to beat. But after I kept tabs on everyone. Everyone was getting married, moving across the country, getting jobs, ya-da ya-da ya-da...while I...was stuck at home. the most of the world

I'd seen in seven years was the pavement where the driveway started to the three miles it took to get into town. I was punished. Punished for something I had no control over... and everyone just moved on. Left me behind, forgot about me. And they said it was easy—don't let your past dictate you—HOW AM I SUPPOSED TO LET GO OF THE PAST WHEN IT'S WRITTEN ON MY FACE?!"

"You ask me why? Why, Jesse? Because they didn't deserve to move on. If my life ended that day, so would everyone else's."

Rhodes, as a moment of sympathy, took off his coat and rolled up his sleeves. The scars revealed, he spat the table. "We didn't move on. We learned to cope. Most of us, at least. Don't think I don't go to sleep with the flames still burning inches from my face. And the man who was never caught. I still remember—we all do."

"You share in my pain. You share in my anger. You're just one bad day away from being just like me. Just like me, Jesse."

Rhodes' phone started buzzing in his pocket.

"There it is!" Davis chuckled with a wheeze.

Rhodes picked up the phone to hear the sound of a distressed Wolfe, "Jesse...you got to get back here, now!" Wolfe hung up the phone.

Rhodes lowered the phone, "What did you do?"

Jonathan Davis looked up with a smirk. "Go see."

Police lights were visible from miles away. Rhodes ran back into the church passing by cops with heavy faces. Quickly he blasted back up the burned stairs that nearly collapsed under his weight. A throng of police crowded around a single room on the second floor. Rhodes remembered it as the old daycare room. When they saw Rhodes enter the from the stairwell they cleared the way. Their faces were just as heavy and concerned.

Wolfe waited for him in the room. His eyes were heavy like boulders, but Jesse paid no mind to them. Rhodes' attention was immediately drawn to what was sitting directly behind the detective.

She'd been there quite some time. Slouched over, bound at the wrists by rope, a body sat in a wooden chair. The white tank top the girl wore was brown and black with decay and vomit. Her skin was an oily green while her hair was black and hung down covering her face.

Rhodes looked down at the girl's arms clinching his hands; he turned red with nausea. From her forearms crawling up to her shoulders she'd been injected with needles. Jonathan Davis didn't even bother to extract them from her body. Track marks riddled her decaying skin, some needles had found their way to the floor and her vomit-soaked lap.

The silence in the room was thick just like the smell was from the rotting flesh. Rhodes looked up at Wolfe while dozens of eyes gazed at him with heavy hearts. The young detective took an exaggerated breath. He approached the girl slouched over in the chair. He couldn't tell who she was, but her presence that still lingered struck him as all too familiar. He grew faint, his skin turned white. With a single mustered nerve, Rhodes tilted the girl's head back. Her mouth was open, a ring of dried puke around the lips. Rhodes screamed and staggered back, his eyes aghast, his spirit for the first time felt a feeling... and that feeling was heartbreak.

"A-Allaura!" Rhodes cried out to the corpse. "Oh...GOD--Allaura!" Jesse kept crying her name. His knees weakened, his face flushed red and his eyes spat rivers of sorrow. "Fuck! Oh my God!" He tried to wrap his arms around the body in shock. Wolfe grabbed him before he could touch the corpse again. Jesse struggled, cops came up behind him, pulling him away.

"NO!" Rhodes with all his might fought away the policemen trying to restrain him. "THAT SON OF A BITCH! No!" His body grew weak from the tears he cried. He fell to his face at the feet of Allaura. Dirty needles spread around him, he didn't care if he touched them. His face was buried in the water of grief and drowned in all the words left unsaid. If she was listening from Heaven above, all he wished for her to hear was, "I'm sorry," he wept.

The Old Detective stood over him. His jaw was heavy. He couldn't help but sympathize in Rhodes' pain. He knew what it was like seeing his beloved after her final moments; too late to save the day. His eyes were watery, his bags sunk to the floor. A part of him wanted to cry out to the God of the burned church just to ask him *Why? Why all this?* But the question never made it to the gates, same as him.

...

The Silver-Faced Ripper, Jonathan Davis was left lingering in that interrogation room. The broken bone in his arm throbbed, he moved very little, but the pain didn't bother him that much; he'd felt worse torment. He kept his head down, eyes pointed, in the same position when Rhodes left. Like a hawk and his prey laid in his lap, he did not break his concentration. Jonathan's deranged mind's eye imagined the look on that poor boy's face when he saw his love and lady dead and defamed in that little, wooden chair. The idea of him screaming and crying and spitting up on himself looking upon the helpless woman who he'd failed to protect...it gave him comfort.

Thinking about it...brought Jonathan great joy. The feral killer broke his concentration with a slight chuckle. Then the abrupt break snowballed into an overwhelming fit of hysterical laughter and painful coughing. Jonathan Davis knew he'd won.

23

The "See you again" After the "Goodbye"

The waves across Lake Thunderbird swayed slowly up to the shoreline of red mud. The water was undisturbed, the sun was just raising to a new day. The blue hues glistened off the lake water bringing in the dawn as if it were ordained my God.

An older man with silver beard and thick glasses drove his easel in the dirt and places a white canvas on its stand. His brushes and his paints and extra canvases sat in a bag at his feet. With every stroke on the white he brought to life the calmness of the ocean against a morning's horizon.

Only a bird's chirp interrupted his concentration; the day was so calm. In the distance, a man in a black coat and a black suit, with a blacker soul came and sat at the shoreline. A cigarette between his fingers drew a single strain of smoke while he looked over the water deep in the dispair of his own thoughts. With a sigh, he turned to his right and saw the man, there, stroking paint to the canvas.

He gazed at the painter with envy. He wished he'd had such a talent, as it were, to free him—if even for a moment—from the vile, disgusting world around him he'd grown to only hate. As if the world had already fallen to rubble, he saw the painter's eyes were full of life and energy...he wished he knew the feeling.

Something drew him to the painter. A heaviness in his gut compelled him to walk up to the man. He threw the cigarette into the water and slowly walked toward him. As he drew closer that early morning the painter only glanced at him for a moment. In a flash he struck his brush into the blue mixed with black and precisely vandalized the canvas with its vibrant hues.

The man in the coat waved his hands to show he meant no harm. With the chill from the water turning his face pale, he asked the painter a simple question, "What else can you paint?"

The painter glanced over his shoulder at the younger man in the black suit and black coat. "For twenty dollars," he said, "I'll paint you just about anything you want."

The man dug in his pockets for his wallet. He unfolded the leather binding and pulled out the only bill he had: a fifty-dollar bill. He handed it to the painter, placing it between his fingers. The painter observed it for a moment then took another canvas and placed it atop the other one on the easel. "What can I do ya for?" asked the painter.

The man looked out over the lake, then as he thought more deeply his head pointed towards the sky. "Paint me a log cabin. A cabin in the woods with a green tin roof. A long porch that wraps from one end to the other. Grass as lush as the trees surrounding the house, and flowers the same color as her eyes. Put her on the front porch at the very top of the stairs in a white, cotton dress. Her black hair flowing all the way down her back, and her eyes piercing through the canvas. Make it remind me of the first time I ever laid eyes on her."

The painter looked at Jesse Rhodes with longing eyes. He could hear the slight shakiness in his voice; the painter knew all too well the pain he felt.

He began with the trees, then the grass, then the house with the porch going all the way around. He took his time on the woman in the white dress. He made sure the detail was placed with such elegance that his buyer would see the lengths he went to fulfill his request. When he reached a stopping point, as Jesse watched the water dance, he broke the quiet, "Son, where can I put you in his picture?"

Jesse Rhodes kept his eyes pointed at the water. A tear fell from his eye as the sun grew brighter at the passing of the morning. Finally, he said with a heavy heart, "Paint me in her arms. I want to be there, again."

The painter continued on. After a while, Jesse sat down burying his head in his knees as well as his grief. He continued there for another hour, then got up.

The painter was still in the midst of the painting, Rhodes threw down his business card and bid the man a far well. "Bring it to my office, if you would," then he left the lake leaving the painter sharing in his grief.

It been a week since the funeral, still everyday Jesse went and visited her gravesite. They buried her right next to her father just a yard away. With every visit Jesse did nothing more than just cry. Each time he'd try to muster up some words, the emotions he hadn't felt in seven years arose and overwhelmed his being.

Jesse stared down at the tombstone with her angel-given name carved into the center. He took shallow breaths trying to not fall down in tears an eighth time. He was the only person in the graveyard, anything he wanted to say was between him and her.

"We all deserved better than this. But you...you deserved it that much more, Allaura. Through it all, you stepped up, not just for yourself...for our daughter. When you couldn't do it for yourself, you did it for her and that was something I could never figure out how do to. She has your eyes—you know that. I see so much of her in you and it's killing me that she has to grow up without you, now. You deserved so much better than this."

Jesse turned pale. He took a moment to regain his composure while the gravestone stared back at him with longing eyes. "You're all that I've never known. Hopefully the stories they told us were true so one day I'll see you again. That'll be the day. That'll be the day. I'm going to avenge you, Allaura."

The Young Detective stood there for a moment and gazed at her for one last time. With rivers falling into the pools of despair, he stumbled away weeping, weeping for his lost Allaura.

24

Silencing of Trumpets

The wind blew Rhodes' hair into his face intertwining with his glasses. The cigarette he smoked warmed his lungs while the early-winter's breeze chilled his face. His coat reeked of past cigarettes; he'd developed the habit almost overnight. He needed something to ease his pain as well as his mind.

Rhodes stood alone outside the Lexington State Prison, he leaned up against the barb-wire fence just next to brick guard tower. The Young Detective looked out across the parking lot; a black truck drove up with Comanche license plates. The truck parked crooked in the spot and an old man whipped out of the driver's side. Jesse seen his face before except with a lot less beard and a lot less hair on top.

Wolfe and Rhodes hadn't spoken since that night at the old, burned church. Both men, by order of the state, were put on an extended leave after receiving metals of bravery by the governor himself. It didn't matter how many days ticked by for either of them, they were anything but past what all took place. Wolfe closed his door, slowly. His eyes were fixed on the young man housing a cigarette between his lips. He walked towards him, stepping onto the sidewalk in front of the guard tower. He snugged his hands in his tweed coat pockets to evade the chill.

"Kid," he said in a low voice.

Jesse exhaled the deathly smoke and nodded his head. "I didn't think you'd come here for this, Wolfe."

"I wouldn't let you have to do this, alone, Kid." Wolfe scoffed then turned to look at the entrance of the prison. Through a gated walkway, two guards and a man in a gray suit were walking out to greet the two detectives.

The man in gray tweed was Warden Damarius Roberts. He was a man a half a decade older than Wolfe but walked just as heavily as Buck. His voice was tainted to a sharp rasp by the decades of cigar smoke.

Wolfe and Rhodes met him at the front gate, men in the guard towers looming over them with sniper rifles in hand. "He ain't talked since he's been here." said the Warden.

A chill went up Rhodes' spine. His eyes slowly found themselves staring at the ground as if to avoid being in the present moment. He still saw Allaura's body every day. The cries from her family when he had to tell them still rung off loudly in his ears.

"We got 'em ready for ya," the old man pointed at the young man with his eyes fixated on his.

Wolfe glanced over at Rhodes, "Are you sure about this, Jesse?"

"No, but I guess that doesn't really matter."

Mr. Damarius Roberts waved them back into the cold depths of the prison. They entered through a brick building where another guard awaited them to sign them in.

"Weapons, please—any personal belongings." said the guard.

Wolfe reached in all his pockets. His hands emerged with his wallet, keys, and smart phone. Rhodes took out those same items but adding a six-shooter to the mix. Both men in single-file stepped through the metal detector—they were both cleared of any contraband.

Rhodes stayed in the back behind Wolfe, the Warden and the two guards. The narrow hallway was crowded with officers filing in and out making their way through the prison.

Jesse fell behind the pack a bit. A single guard scooted past the Warden and Wolfe. He turned his head around as he passed his boss and tried to greet him in a rush. He was still walking forward with his head turned back; he unintentionally shoulder-checked Rhodes. "I'm so sorry!" the guard exclaimed. Rhodes kept walking forward, waving at the man as if to say he was forgiven. The Young Detective fell back in line with the pack.

The Warden stopped in front of a metal door. There was no slit to peek inside. "He's in here--Wolfe and I will be watching through the glass. We've got your back, Detective Rhodes." Mr. Roberts assured him giving him a wink and a half-smile.

Rhodes' face stayed stern and cold like the air outside. His eyes fixed on the door. Wolfe and Mr. Roberts eyed him, then eyed each other.

"You got this, kid," said Wolfe.

"Open Door A-12!" Warden commanded.

An alarm sounded off, Wolfe and the Warden stepped away from the door; Jesse pushed the heavy door open with no hesitation and entered the brick room.

On the right wall was the two-way glass. In the center of the room a deformed man in an orange jumpsuit, legs and arms restrained, sat slouched over in a metal chair. His eyes were wide open and didn't break concentration when the door swung open. Davis was like a still beast.

Rhodes walked around the table, he stood, looming over the burned killer. He just eyed him for a moment; how still he was—his calmness—made him sense frustration. He thought the ripper would lash out at any moment, just waiting for the right time to instigate madness. Rhodes didn't care whether he was agitated or not, he was to control the situation, not some psychopath.

"I figured you'd ask to see me sooner," Davis said as the door swung open. He looked up, hands cuffed in front of him, and waved at Jesse. "I hope you're in good spirits."

"When?"

"When what? You'll have to be more specific."

"When did you take her?"

"Cutting right to the chase, I see," Jonathan leaned back, "are you sure you don't want to engage in a little small-talk before we talk--"

Rhodes struck Davis across the face. He fell sideways nearly out of his chair. Davis rose back up, slowly, with a squinted smirk on his face. "Do you really want to know?"

Rhodes' silence spoke loudly.

"I picked her up when she was leaving your save house." Davis finally said.

Rhodes couldn't bear to hear it. He tried to maintain himself, but his eyes bawled with tears. "Son of a bitch," he muttered.

"She was resilient. I know that means a lot for people to hear," said Davis, "she told me for months how you were going to catch me."

"Months?"

"Yeah. Months."

"You injected her with so much heroin. It wasn't even in her veins. It was just pooled under her skin." Rhodes spoke through the tears.

"By the end she was practically begging for it," Davis replied, "Would you like to hear her last words?"

Rhodes' silence, once again, spoke loudly.

"'*One...more...hit.*'" Davis leaned forward and smiled up.

"Oh, God!" Rhodes crumbled over the table.

Wolfe and the warden looked through the glass. Wolfe could share in his pain. Knowing what it was like for their women to be taken away by this man...it was an unimaginable pain.

"That was who she was, Jesse. That's what the fire made her into. It wasn't my choices, it was her own. I was just...guiding her back to her true self."

"We're not all scumbags like you, Jonathan. You're worse than whoever started that fire."

"Remember what I said the first time we met in a room like this? You're just like me deep down. Well, on the outside you're not too far off."

"You think everyone is scum like you," replied Rhodes, "You're a coward who couldn't live with his own self-loathing that you forced it on the rest of us."

"Maybe so," said Davis, "Maybe I am just a madman. But why should they go on living when my life ended? I'm a dead man. A dead man with a paintbrush. What do dead men paint? They paint the picture they always wanted to. I wanted this more than anything! The look on all their bullshit faces...I scared them. They pushed me to the side and forgot I existed, and they grew to fear me. Like all men should."

"Now you're back to nothing, Jonathan. Everything you did amounted to nothing."

"Is that what you think? All I did was nothing? Even though what I did was a defining moment in so many people's lives. So many outlooks and perceptions changed because of me! They will never forget me and my shadow will cast over this shithole for years to come. I'm locked up and people still lock their doors with thoughts of me!"

"You still could've had a life, Jonathan."

"You know, I always imagined myself living on a beach. I deserved to live on a beach. California, perhaps? Something... *away* from it all. Maybe you're right it all could've been different. Where did you imagine your life going?"

"I wanted to pursue music. It was always a knack of mine. I actually picked back up on writing verses again, but it doesn't come naturally to me, anymore."

"I think I remember hearing you sing, once."

"Probably when we all got together on Wednesday nights."

"Remember when Tony Dillon flooded the toilet while Pastor Rick was preaching?"

"Yeah. When we finished the hallway was covered in water. That was a strange night."

"I couldn't stop laughing. We all had to go out of the fire exit it was so bad."

The two started laughing.

"I had to carry Allaura on my back. She'd just bought new jeans; she didn't want to ruin them."

"Man... if it had never happened."

"But it did."

"I stole...I stole the case files from Ellis' safe. They were in my house when y'all--"

"I have them, Jonathan."

"Have you looked at them?"

"Every day."

"It drove me insane. I tried to put the pieces together, but I couldn't look...I couldn't actually see all of it, again. Only the images in my head from what I could remember."

"What do you remember from that night?"

"The heat. The screaming. *My screaming.* What it feels like to have your skin melt off. That's all I can stand to remember, without losing complete control of me own sanity."

"It's always in the back of my mind even when I'm thinking on something else. It's always...looming."

"Is it loud? Does it thump at the back on your mind?"

"Like trumpets."

"Will you avenge us, Jesse?"

"Avenge you?"

"No. Not me. Avenge the rest of them."

"I plan to."

Rhodes stood up and walked around the table and leaned against Jonathan's side. "How loud are the trumpets now?"

"Loud!"

"Good, then. Let me tell you something that might soothe your mind: I keep having this reoccurring dream. It's the same every time, the details wonder, but it's always the same..."

"I'm alone—stranded in the woods. I'm looking around, but it's too dark to see anything. Then suddenly I hear the trotting of a horse. Coming at me is an Indian warrior. I'm afraid, but I don't move. The warrior stops in front of me and looks into my eyes. He asks me, 'Why does a warrior cry? Why does a warrior cry?'"

"Why? Why does a warrior cry?"

"I don't know. I'd always wake up. But when I was visiting Allaura's grave, the answer hit me."

"Why does a warrior cry?"

"...Because he's seen too much."

Rhodes pulled out the gun the cop in the hallways planted on him and pulled the trigger on Jonathan Davis. He fell sideways with the blood and skin splattering off his temple. Before he hit the ground the alarms sounded all throughout the prison.

Rhodes walked out of the room, cops running up and down the hall. He stepped into the center, the cop who bumped him earlier came back around and finished the exchange, taking the gun off him. Wolfe and the warden darted into the hallway; Rhodes walked away from them. Though the prison was going on lockdown, the cell keeper unbarred the door for Rhodes and let him out. The sound of sirens alarmed all of Lexington: the young detective had gotten his revenge.

...

Night was falling over Norman. The news had already shattered of Davis's death in prison. Jesse listened as police sirens enriched the sunset's atmosphere from the rooftop of Police Headquarters building. The cold was even more blistering up there. Alone with his thoughts, blood now drying on his hand, he was enslaved by his own thoughts.

The door opened behind him, he wasn't expecting company. Rhodes didn't bother to turn around and greet the figure. Alas, the figure came and stood beside him looking over the ledge.

Wolfe didn't have the guts to look the kid in the face. He stared blankly over the ledge at the line of cars, trees, and druggies lining the street. "I suppose I'm next," he muttered.

Rhodes waited to give a response. He let the thick chill of the wind nip at his neck while the pale pink sky turned into an unforgiving hazy black. "You want to die, don't you, Wolfe?"

The Old Detective didn't give too much time to ponder the thought. "Yes," he said in a low whisper.

"Do it yourself, then." Rhodes looked over the ledge out at the fallen city as he spoke. The thought occurred to him, if he'd just been born anywhere else, in maybe just one town over, none of this would've happened. He wouldn't have to live on with all the grief and pain Norman had caused him. He pondered, if Wolfe were to jump off that roof at that moment, and Rhodes were to witness his fall to his death...he wouldn't blame him. In some ways, he would've envied him for realizing death had better to offer than life.

    Rhodes walked away and headed off the roof to leave Wolfe to his own devices. He wished him all the luck the world had to offer them, but with their experience, it wasn't much to give.

    Rhodes thought as he swung open the door, sirens blasting, cicadas singing, druggies blasting poison into their arm, Natives sieging back land by force, children starving, mothers crying, fathers breaking their backs for a silver coin...he looked back as he was in the doorway and thought to himself:

    If God is in control...he isn't.

    Rhodes let the door slam behind him. Before he left the fourth floor, he unclipped his badge from his belt buckle and placed it on Wolfe's desk. He officially resigned his mantle as The Young Detective.

Epilogue

Look what I've done. My actions. <u>NO</u> amount of good deeds will undo what I did. If only I wasn't such a coward.

The detective... he'll come for me, soon. He won't let up until he pulls me into the light.

I won't let him find me. I can't let him find me.

He won't win. I'll win. I'll survive like I've survived this entire time.

Hide and seek. I always win hide and seek.

If I just stay in my hiding spot, hold my breath in my palms, stay still. Just stay still.

That detective will never know it was me who set the fire. He'll never know I could've prevented everything from happening if I would just confess.

None of them will ever know it was me.

THE END.

Made in the USA
Coppell, TX
28 February 2024